TWICE AS GOOD
A Reed Haddok Western

TWICE AS GOOD

A Reed Haddok Western

Tom V. Whatley

SUNSTONE
PRESS

SANTA FE

On the Cover: *Cowboy on Horseback* by Howard Schleeter

Sunstone books may be purchased for educational, business, or sales promotional
use. For information please write: Special Markets Department, Sunstone Press,
P.O. Box 2321, Santa Fe, New Mexico 87504-2321.

Library of Congress Cataloging-in-Publication Data:

Whatley, Tom V., 1940-
    Twice as good : a Reed Haddok western / Tom V. Whatley.
      p. cm.
    ISBN 0-86534-463-9 (pbk. : alk. paper)
    1. Haddok, Reed (Fictitious character)—Fiction. I. Title.

PS3573.H33T88 2005
813'.54—dc22

                                2005019004

WW.SUNSTONEPRESS.COM
SUNSTONE PRESS / POST OFFICE BOX 2321 / SANTA FE, NM 87504-2321 /USA
(505) 988-4418 / *ORDERS ONLY* (800) 243-5644 / FAX (505) 988-1025

For my friends G. Rick Hall
and the late Rick Murphy.
Together they were twice as good.

1

A wicked blow threw his head to the side. Reed Haddok was helpless, his hands locked behind him and his legs tied to the bottom of the chair. Blood was streaming down his face.

"You're not so bad now, Haddok," Loyd Beecham said with a sarcastic chuckle.

Beecham was sitting across the room enjoying the beating his battered enemy was getting at the hand of his henchman.

"If you'll beg a little, I'll tell him to stop," Beecham added.

Haddok only stared at him through eyes almost swollen shut.

Beecham nodded and the beating continued with cruel accuracy. Haddok blacked out but it did not stop the blows. They continued until Beecham called the man off.

The once frightened Beecham was now in control. He got up and walked over, taking Haddok by his hair and lifting his head. He smiled, then turned to walk away. Stopping at the door, he spoke over his shoulder without looking back, "Kill him."

The jolt of the stagecoach jarred Loyd Beecham back to reality. He enjoyed thinking such thoughts. Why couldn't they be real.

2

The road was rocky and rough. The bouncing stage kept the four passengers in the air more than in their seats. Loyd Beecham completely ignored the other three men traveling with him. He did so for two reasons. He didn't want anybody asking him questions and formulating a memory of him to tell others. And he was also trying to use the time to finalize a plan he had been working on for a long time.

Beecham had left the Prescott area of Arizona a beaten and frightened man. Reed Haddok robbed him of a dream and it had cost him plenty. The highest part of the cost was his own sense of safety. His fear of Haddok was the heart of a plan to kill him. He had about decided no amount of money and hired killers could accomplish that. His use of a carefully planned alias and reputation in Santa Fe provided him with a brief time of security. Using a lifelong sense of anticipating the future, he felt it was just a matter of time until Haddok showed up in Santa Fe. The last thing he wanted was to face him again.

He was relieved to be away from Santa Fe. His fear of Haddok had grown so much he imagined him showing up at any moment. But he knew it would happen sooner or later. Will Malone had been right. He was running. It really didn't matter that Malone knew he was afraid. Malone was like all the other people in his life. He could always hire another Will Malone.

His plan was to get to the Two Butte ranch near Fort Defiance.

He had bought the ranch some time back under the name Jake Lanceford. For a man always looking for a place to hide, the ranch had been just what he would need. Once there, he would surround himself with the best gunmen he could hire and stay behind them until he learned Haddok was dead. He would then lead the gunslingers back to Prescott and claim what was rightfully his.

The ranch and a clean name was waiting for him. Lanceford had been a pal of his back in New Orleans and wouldn't mind him using his name, if he was still alive. Most of Beecham's friends back there were not. He had eight men on the payroll at the ranch to keep up the ruse of it being a working ranch. They all were wanted men, but there wasn't a gunslinger in the bunch. At least he knew they would all kill for money.

His stage trip from Santa Fe to Fort Defiance gave him time to think. The ranch would be an easy place to defend. His biggest need to make it work was men good with a gun. He thought of all the people he could count on for help. He finally settled on Logan Franks. Franks was an old friend and knew the kind of men he needed. Franks had been hanging out for over three years in the Bend area of Kansas.

Beecham dug out a pencil and a piece of paper. Trying to time the bounces of the coach, he scribbled a note.

> Logan,
> I need all the good guns you can find. The pay will be good and I'll throw in a bonus. Send them to Two Butte ranch a half day ride north of Fort Defiance. I'll be using the name Jake Lanceford. Don't tell them my real name. I'll owe you and will settle up with you later. Don't let me down. I needed them yesterday.
> Loyd Beecham

He folded the note and slipped it in his pocket. He would send it toward Kansas the first chance he had.

The best thing that could happen for Beecham would be to learn Haddok was dead. Something inside him kept saying he was alive. He tried to sleep on the bouncing coach. It wouldn't let him. It didn't bother him though. When he didn't sleep, he didn't dream about Haddok.

The stage pulled into San Mateo late in the afternoon on the second day out of Santa Fe. Beecham and the other passengers were told they would have a couple of hours to freshen up and eat.

Beecham went inside and inquired of the stage operator concerning the next stage heading back toward Santa Fe. He learned one would leave the next morning. He found an envelope and addressed it to Logan Franks, River Bluff Saloon, Bend, Kansas. He handed the letter to the operator and asked him to put it in the mailbag on the next morning's stage. He then walked to the café down the street to get some food. As he walked, he thought, I hope Franks can get me some men heading my way fast.

Beecham sat down at a table alone and enjoyed the first good food in two days. His thoughts never left Haddok for long. He was anxious to get tucked in at the ranch and surround himself with a barrier of protection to at least keep Haddok at a distance. Too much time had passed since he put the big price on Haddok's head. He now felt his plan to have him killed wouldn't work. He also felt it was just a matter of time until Haddok would get to Will Malone. Malone's name was out there with the offer to kill Haddok. Haddok would not let that ride forever. Malone was the only person who could tie him to the Fort Defiance area. For that reason and the fact he felt like Malone would talk under pressure, he had to get to the Two Butte ranch without attracting any attention. He wanted no one to be able to place him there.

He climbed onto the stagecoach and settled in for another long leg of the journey. He felt like every mile of the trip was taking him away from Haddok, even though he knew in his heart that it was taking him closer to him.

3

Fort Defiance was a typical army garrison. With the soldiers came all the people who used the men as a means of making money. A semblance of a town sprang up early on and at the present offered all the amenities needed from whiskey to women. Stores and saloons were doing a bristling business. The fort sat along one of the routes west over the continental divide and served as a good resupply point for people heading west. One of the things Beecham liked about the place was that so many new faces were usually in the town. The local people figured they were all headed west and paid little attention to detail about them. Beecham was betting on nobody remembering his face.

The stage pulled into the settlement late in the day, five days out of Santa Fe. Beecham planned on getting out of town as quickly as possible. His only tie to the area was under the name Jake Lanceford and he was determined to avoid using it this trip.

He stepped off the stage, waited until his bags were lowered to the ground, and headed straight for the livery. He bargained for a riding horse and saddle. He also bought a pack horse and pack. He told the hostler he was heading west. With his bags on the pack horse, he led both animals to a hitching rail outside a small café. He walked in and ordered a good meal of steak and beans. He ate alone and offered no conversation with any of the patrons. It appeared nobody was paying him any attention. That was good. When he finished, he paid up and walked outside. He stepped into the saddle and rode out of town as if he was headed west. When he was well away from the settlement he circled until he hit the road heading north. It would lead him to the Two Buttes ranch.

He rode well into the night before stopping to sleep a while. He made a dry camp off from what was no more than wagon ruts across hard ground.

He was in the saddle when the sun came up. He judged he had about three more hours of riding before he would get to the ranch. In his mind he couldn't get there fast enough. Something kept telling him trouble was on his heels. He knew full well that trouble would be Haddok. If he could get to the ranch and get ready for him, just maybe he could stop the endless string of nightmares he had endured since leaving Prescott.

The ranch house sat back at the base of one of two almost identical buttes. The buttes, like ancient sentinels, stood almost five hundred feet above the level of the land. He knew he had been on land he owned long before he saw the ranch buildings in the distance. He had ridden out of the timber in the bottom and rode uphill to top out and see the giant buttes. The land lay before him as small rolling hills with only scrub trees dotting the landscape. The buttes stood like two powerful giants. From his vantage point he could see the ranch buildings and a small ribbon of smoke rising from the main house. Another hour of riding brought him up to the gate standing about six hundred paces from the house.

Beecham was surprised no one was in sight. He had hoped to find the place in good shape and guarded. Those were his instructions. But the men he left to look after the ranch were a strange lot. There was not a cowhand in the bunch. He figured the cattle had certainly been neglected, but that didn't matter. He didn't buy the place to raise cattle. He needed a hiding place that could be easily defended and Two Buttes ranch was such a place.

The men included two brothers, Cliff and Ross Partain. They were bad and would do anything for money. Beecham had left them in charge. The others he knew only by last names. There was a

Peeden, Foster, Fullmer, Bledso, and Gray. The eighth was a Mexican named Estrada. The Partain brothers had rounded them up for Beecham and told him they were good for the job.

Setting his horse at the gate, Beecham waited a minute to see if anyone challenged him. He saw no one. He stepped down, opened the gate, led his horses through, then stepped back into the saddle to ride on up to the house. Horses were in the corral but there was no sign of a living human being. Beecham was clearly puzzled.

He tied his horses and stepped up on the porch. He turned the knob and pushed the door open. What he saw made him sick. The place was in shambles. Whiskey bottles and trash littered the floor. His gallant band of defenders were sprawled all over the main room. It appeared they were all sleeping off a drunk.

"I'm going to take my horses to the barn," he shouted. "You ain't got long. Get up and clean your belongings and trash out of my house. If it ain't done by the time I get back, I'll bury you on this place."

They looked at him with the fuzzy headed stare of surprise as he stormed out.

4

Beecham unloaded his bags from the pack horse and dropped them on the porch. He then led the animals to the corral where he unsaddled his horse, removed the pack rack from the other, and turned them into the corral. He threw them some hay over the fence and headed back to the house. He took a seat on the porch and listened to the furor inside as the men scurried around cleaning up the place. The chore took about an hour as he watched them drag their gear to the bunkhouse. Finally, they stood before him and declared they were through.

"From now on you enter my house when I invite you. Do you understand?" Beecham said.

They all nodded. They were a pitiful looking sight. Beecham thought, I'm in big trouble if this is what I've got protecting me.

"Ross, you stay here. The rest of you get out of my sight," Beecham said as he fished some paper out of his pocket and began to write. When he finished, he looked at Ross Partain and said, "I chose you because you look to be in the best shape. I want you to take the buckboard and go into town. Buy us these provisions." Beecham handed him the list and some money. "Look around and see if you can find somebody who can cook. Bring whoever you find, man or woman. I'll pay twenty dollars a week. That ought to get somebody out here."

Partain said, "Sure thing boss."

"I also want you to go by the stage office and tell them you are expecting a letter addressed to Frank Lain. It probably won't be there, but I'm going to need you to go to town every few days to check and see if it has arrived."

"Frank Lain. Okay boss. I got it," Partain said.

"I don't want any of the rest of the men in town until I tell you. I want somebody on the high ground behind the ranch during daylight every day. Do it til I tell you different. Put somebody on the gate day and night. Tell your brother Cliff to work out the schedule while you are gone and get them busy. I don't want anybody getting to this ranch house without me letting them. There will be some more men showing up here in the next few weeks to help me. If they say they've been sent by Logan Franks, let them come on in. Otherwise, I don't care what you do to whoever shows up. You got any questions?"

Ross Partain was hung over, but even in his condition he recognized his boss was serious and what he seemed to be saying was he was afraid somebody was coming after him. "I don't mean to be nosy Mr. Lanceford, but it appears you got somebody on your tail. I sure would like to know what I'm getting into."

"You've been drawing my money for a while and it appears I've been paying you to get drunk and do nothing. I assure you I will call on you to do no more than what I've just told you."

"Fair enough," Partain answered.

"Then get at it."

Beecham began moving his gear inside as Partain walked away. He thought, I hope Franks gets me some help here fast. I'd hate for Haddok to show up now.

The next couple of days Beecham spent getting settled in. He didn't sleep much the first night. He didn't feel safe and fought to stay awake. He took cat naps the next day. The last thing he needed was a bad dream. Night two was better. He slept most of the night and did not dream. Night three was horrible. When he came out of the nightmare, Haddok had a knife against his throat. The men he had around him did not help. The Partain brothers were the only ones he felt like he could depend upon, and he wasn't sure about them. He thought seriously about saddling up and riding out. He knew without a doubt his only hope was in Logan Franks. He hoped the men were on their way.

5

A month had passed since Beecham's arrival at Two Buttes. The men on the ranch were actually doing better than he expected. The guards were holding down their posts and no visitors had shown up at the ranch. He personally checked them at different intervals during the day and night to make sure they were on their toes.

Ross Partain returned from his first trip into town with a cook by the name of Woods. He had worked as cook for a number of outfits. He wasn't great, but he beat not having one. The older Partain had continued to make weekly trips into Fort Defiance for provisions and to check on the awaited message from Will Malone. The letter had not come.

The first of the gunfighters sent by Logan Franks arrived on a Tuesday about noon. He was brought up to the house by Cliff Partain. He introduced himself as Burl Isom. He looked a little old for a gunfighter. Looks didn't matter. Beecham had heard about Isom before and the reputation was what he liked. Isom was reported to be fast with a gun and plain mean.

"The name's Jake Lanceford," Beecham said. "Swing down and let's talk a spell."

Isom stepped down from the saddle, stretched a bit, and said, "Logan tells me you need some help and I'm for hire if the price is right."

"I'll pay you a hundred a month. When the others get here, and I hope there's some more coming, I'll fill you in on the job. I'll also tell you about the bonus that's out there for you."

"Sounds good to me. There ain't been much work back in Kansas."

"Good. Put your gear in that bunkhouse," Beecham said. "Supper will be ready at five o'clock. Get yourself settled in and I'll see you then."

Isom headed for the bunkhouse and Beecham began to feel a little better.

The next morning four more gunfighters rode in about nine o'clock. They all looked on the young side.

"I'm Jake Lanceford," Beecham said as he walked out to meet them. Isom saw them ride up and walked over to greet them. They seemed like old friends.

"I'm Lewis Garron," a lanky man said from beneath what looked like a five day beard. "This here is Wade Harper." He nodded to the man on his left. Harper made an impression on Beecham because when he looked toward the gunslinger, he looked into the eyes of a cold man whose face reflected no emotion at all. Garron turned toward the two men setting the horses behind him. "This is Toby Horton." He motioned to the man on the right. "This gent is Wiley Pounds," he said, nodding toward the man on the left.

"I've heard about all of you at some time or another. Logan has done me a big favor by sending you out this way. It seems like ya'll already know Isom," Beecham said. A couple of them nodded and grinned when he mentioned Isom. "If you want the job, it's a hundred a month with a bonus I'll tell you about later."

They all looked at each other and Garron spoke. "You've hired yourself some guns. We're ready to go to work. You just tell us what we need to know and we'll get at it."

"That's great," Beecham replied. "Do you know if Logan is sending any more men beside ya'll?"

"He told me to tell you he was sending seven of the best guns anywhere. Looks like five of us are here. There must be two more on the way," Garron said.

"Isom will show you the bunkhouse. We'll wait on the other two. When they get here I'll fill everybody in on my plans. I'm real proud you are here."

They headed toward the bunkhouse and began to move their gear inside. Beecham couldn't help but think about how much having a few good guns around could help a man's disposition. Logan Franks had come through.

The last two gunfighters came in late in the afternoon of the same day. They introduced themselves to Beecham as Benton Walls and Zeke Melton. Both were known gunslingers and the other five were proud to see them arrive. They all had worked together at different times and places over the past few years. The word out on Walls was, despite his youth, he was lightning quick on the draw. Melton, on the other hand, was known for his down home ways, calm demeanor, and skill with a gun. The fact he was alive was evidence enough that he was quick on the draw

All seven men were talking and kidding each other about old times when Beecham interrupted. "Supper is at five. After supper I'll lay out my plans for you."

They led the two latest arrivals to the bunkhouse and helped them get settled in. Beecham went back into the house and told the cook to set the table for eight.

The gunslingers made it to the ranch house a little early and as soon as the food was put on the table they began to wolf down the beef stew and bread. They were all seated around one big table with Beecham at the head.

Benton Walls broke the casual talk with a question to Zeke Melton. "Zeke, did you hear the news that the Malone feller doing the talking for the Beecham feller back in Santa Fe got hisself killed?"

"Nope. But it don't surprise me none. If Haddok is as good as they say, I figured it was just a matter of time fore he looked Malone up," Melton replied.

Loyd Beecham had a look of shock on his face. He hid it quickly. "What happened?" Beecham asked.

"The word is they found him shot somewhere outside of town. He had his pistol in his hand like he was drawing it. Nobody seen or heard nothing," Walls answered.

Beecham turned his thoughts inward. If Malone talked and I'm sure he did, Haddok knows I'm somewhere around Fort Defiance. He could be on his way here right now.

6

Beecham was quiet until the men finished eating and the cook had taken the food and dishes off the table. When they were alone, he began revealing his plans.

"Men, I want to fill you in on what is happening here. My name is not Jake Lanceford. He's a friend of mine from back in New Orleans and I used his name to buy this place. My name is Loyd Beecham." He was nervous and his revelation got the gunslingers attention. He continued, "When Walls told about the death of Will Malone, I figured I'd better tell you the truth. I fully expected Haddok to be dead by now and I wanted you men to go with me back to Prescott and help me reclaim my property there. Now it looks like I'm gonna need you to keep Haddok at a distance. I want you to kill him and keep him from killing me. Do you have a problem with that?"

Garron spoke up quickly. "So you are Beecham. Did Logan know that?"

"Yes. We go way back. I asked him not to tell you. I've been trying to stay under cover until Haddok is dead."

"Tell us about Haddok," Wiley Pounds said. "I knew some of the men you had with you in Arizona. I'd done a couple of jobs with Sledge. He was good with a gun. I heard Haddok beat him to the draw. Is that right?"

"Yes, it's true. Haddok is good with a gun and he is tough. That's why I asked Logan to send me good men. I assume all of you can handle yourself in a gunfight," Beecham answered.

The gunslingers looked at each other a little more seriously now.

"You don't have to worry about that. There's not a man here who's afraid of Haddok," Walls said. "Do you know where Haddok is now?"

"No. I don't. Malone was the only person in Santa Fe who could tie me to the Fort Defiance area. If it was Haddok who killed him, then he's on his way here. I'm sure Malone talked before he died."

"So, how do you plan for us to work this," Garron asked, quickly assuming the lead man position for the bunch of gunmen.

"I chose this ranch as a place to hide out because it's easy to defend. There's no way that a bunch of men or a single man can slip up on this place. I want you to keep everybody away from the ranch til we learn Haddok's here and then go get him. That's simple enough," Beecham answered.

"It's more than a hundred a month simple," Garron added. "You've had twenty thousand on his head for a spell and it ain't worked. If we do what you want, then it's going to cost you a sight more than a hundred a month."

"I figured as much. I'll give whoever kills him the twenty thousand and five thousand each for the rest of you when it happens," Beecham shot back.

"That's fair enough," Garron said. "Are you men willing to take it for that?"

They nodded agreement with a lot of smiles and thoughts of being rich.

"What about the rest of the men you have here on the ranch? Are they in on this," Garron asked?

"No. They don't know who I am and I want to keep it that way. Every one of them would slit your throat for five dollars but there ain't a gunman in the bunch. They wouldn't be any help with

Haddok. We'll use them to help cover the ranch when you have to be away."

"Do you think Haddok will come alone?" Pounds asked.

"More than likely. The thing you all need to remember is if I get killed, then you don't get paid," Beecham said with a smile.

"You get that money stacked up and ready to pay us," Toby Horton said. Horton probably was the fastest one of the seven with the draw and he intended to be the one who made the twenty thousand. "We'll make sure you're alive to pay us."

"I'm gonna leave how you do it up to you. I know you're good or you wouldn't be here. Just remember, Haddok has killed some good men," Beecham said.

"I been wanting to know something," Wiley Pounds said. "Did Haddok kill Ike Craven?"

"I don't think so," Beecham replied. "I hired Craven to go kill Haddok as soon as I got back to Santa Fe. Somebody shot him way before he got to Prescott. Why do you want to know?"

"I'd seen Craven in action and I'm not sure I ever saw a faster draw. Whoever killed him had to be some kind of quick. I just wondered if it was Haddok," Pounds said.

"I'm sure Haddok couldn't beat Craven," Beecham said. He didn't bother to tell them he had never seen Haddok's fast draw. "It must have been somebody we don't know anything about."

They talked on a spell and then the gunslingers left the house. They had a lot of talking to do before morning. Beecham was glad to have them there. He knew the kind of men they were and he knew the money would keep him safe. He would sleep well tonight.

7

Beecham's gunfighters were among the best in the business. The old man of the group was Burl Isom. Being a fifty three year old gunfighter was proof enough he was good. Isom was known for having a mile wide mean streak. His reputation made his draw faster than it really was. Most people were scared of him.

Wiley Pounds was forty eight. Beecham had heard talk about how fast his draw was. His strength was in his intelligence. He outsmarted most of the men he killed.

The middle aged part of the bunch was made up of Wade Harper, Zeke Melton, and Lewis Garron. Harper was twenty-six, Melton thirty-one, and Garron thirty. Harper was good with a pistol and knife. Melton was a quiet man who was fast on the draw. Garron was different. He was evil. He liked to kill and he liked his reputation. Being in charge was important to him.

The babies of the group were probably the fastest guns. Benton Walls had a blazing draw that left five men dead before he turned nineteen. Toby Horton was twenty-two and he was not afraid of the other six. He knew he was better than the rest. They didn't know it, but it didn't make him any difference. He had a quiet confidence about him that didn't have to do a lot of talking. All he planned on doing was be the one standing when all the shooting stopped.

Since they now knew their boss' real identity and that he wanted them to kill Haddok while protecting him, the hired guns started to map out their plans. Garron, as usual, gravitated to the lead man.

"As I see it, we got two things to take care of," Garron said. "We got to keep Beecham alive til we can kill Haddok. I think our best bet is to keep him here on the ranch."

Wiley Pounds chuckled when he answered, "I don't think you could run him off this ranch til he knows Haddok is dead. He seems mighty scared."

They all nodded in agreement.

Pounds continued, "The ranch will be easy to guard. I've looked it over a little. Three of us can keep anybody away from Beecham during the day. One watching the front, one at the back, and one at the house will do. It gets a little harder at night. One man, if he's good, could slip in close at night."

"I think you're right," Isom said. "We all need to be close at night. I think we need somebody in town during the day to try and find out if Haddok shows up there. I kinda figure he will show up in town first asking questions about Beecham. Maybe a couple of us need to go there every day or so."

"I buy that," Garron said. "Why don't you and Wiley ride into town tomorrow and see what you can find out. We'll get the low down on the area around here and keep Beecham locked down. We can use the men Beecham has working here to fill in some holes if we need to."

They all agreed and decided to have two men at Beecham's quarters during the night. One would be outside and the other inside. Harper and Walls won the first half night shift and walked up to the house to break the news to Beecham. He was happy to have them.

8

Loyd Beecham felt safe for the first time in months. He actually slept all night after his guards arrived. That was a first in a long list of nights filled with bad dreams and fearful wallowing.

The next morning he walked out and called the two Partain brothers over to him. He had already told the men who had been on the ranch all along that they would be taking their orders from Garron and his men. He had other plans for the Partain boys. They were a cut above the other men. Cliff and Ross walked over to where Beecham was standing.

"I've got a little something I want you to do for me and there will be some extra money in it for you if you accept," Beecham said to the two puzzled men. "I want you to keep your eyes and ears open. If you hear of anything I might need to know or if you suspect I'm in any kind of danger, you come straight to me."

They agreed and Beecham left. Cliff was a bit younger than Ross and usually took the lead of his older brother. He held back in the conversation with Beecham and didn't let his real feelings come out until he and his brother were alone.

"Ross, I ain't got this figured out yet," Cliff said. "Lanceford rides in here and gives us this spill about he don't want nobody gettin' to him. Then he brings these gunslingers in to protect him. Now me and you both have had a good look at the bunch he brought in and we both know you probably couldn't look the country over and find anybody better with a gun than what he's got. Now he's tellin' you and me to look out for him too. You know what I think? I think we are crazy for hanging out here. I don't know what's coming and I don't know when, but something is about to happen around here that could sure mess up our good life."

"Now Cliff, you don't go gettin' spooked on me. We're drawing good wages and ain't neither one of us done a days work in over a year," Ross replied.

"Yeah, I know. But ain't no years wages for doin' nuthin' worth my hide. I got this feeling Ross. I say we don't say nuthin' and just ride out of here."

"No. We'll sit tight and see how it shapes up. We'll keep a couple of horses ready and if a storm starts rumblin in, we'll ride out ahead of it."

"I just don't want to wake up in the middle of the night and find out it's already here. I'll listen to you and sit tight, but it's going to be the loose kind of tight," Cliff said. He managed a slight smile when he turned and walked off.

9

Reed Haddok rode away from the Rocking H ranch at daybreak. The morning air was crisp and held back the heat waiting to drift down the valley in a couple of hours.

He was on his way to see Tall Tree and Shining Moon. The last time he had been with them he promised to tell them when he decided to get married. He was not certain Tall Tree's recovery from the gunshot wound was sufficient for him to attend the wedding. He only knew he would keep his promise and let them know.

The journey to their hidden valley was without event. He was careful to check his back trail and he kept to the low ground as much as possible. He saw no sign of any recent travel along his route. Living on the edge was normal for him and he knew how to do it. His care in travel was caused by two things. He never knew when somebody would try to collect the bounty on his head and he certainly planned on keeping their hidden valley a secret. He would die before he would lead someone to his Indian friends.

He reached the mountain side overlooking the waterfall marking the entrance to their valley late in the afternoon. He judged there was about an hour of light left. Leaving his horse in the usual place, he entered the stream well away from the waterfall. He crossed over to the eastern bank and worked his way up the tunnel of brush lining both sides until he came to the final bend in the stream before reaching the waterfall. He walked waist deep in the water and held close to the bank. He came to a halt when he reached the last bend and then began again, slowly working himself around the bend. He carefully checked the area just beneath the falls to make sure no one was around. Certain the area was clear, he crawled up on the bank and slid back into the thick brush. He would wait until dark before he entered the valley. He also wanted to give the lookout, who he was sure had seen him, time to tell the people inside he was coming.

When it had been dark for about an hour he went to the waterfall, staying in the stream, and was under the falling water in a matter of minutes. The cold shock brought back memories of the other times he had entered the valley. Soon he found the narrow passage in the darkness and walked through. He was welcomed on the other side by Tall Tree and his son.

Haddok recognized the voice that came out of the darkness beside the small path. "It is good to have Haddok back at our village."

"I knew you would be here to greet me," Haddok said.

"Come. We will go to my lodge," Tall Tree said as he placed a strong grip on Haddok's shoulder.

They walked silently to the gathering of stone houses. Haddok could see the fires and silhouettes of the people around them as they grew nearer. Shining Moon came to meet them as they approached and Haddok put his strong arms out and hugged her.

"What brings my other Tall Tree to our valley," Shining Moon said as she took his arm and led him to the fireside where all the village was gathered. Haddok took a seat by Shining Moon before he spoke. Tall Tree and his son sat across the fire from them.

"I came to keep my promise. In six moons I will be married. I know well the laws of your valley. I do not wish to bring discord among your people. However, it would please me if my friend Tall Tree and his strong woman Shining Moon could be there." Haddok spoke in a loud voice for all the people to hear. "The marriage will take place at my ranch on the morning of the sixth sunrise."

"So my friend has decided to marry the woman called Samantha?" Tall Tree asked with a smile.

"Yes. She will be a good wife to me like Shining Moon is to you."

"We are honored," Shining Moon said.

"The moon has gone through it's circle since you left us," Tall Tree added. "We have had no Apache visitors near our valley. We have seen no sign of them when we move out from our valley hunting. It is as if they have decided to stay away. Your medicine has worked."

"It was not my medicine. It was the medicine of He Who Runs With Spirits," Haddok said.

"It is good to have my friend here," Tall Tree said. "Bring food and we will eat. Before the night is over the men of the village will talk and decide. I would like for us to be at your marriage. However, I will abide by their wishes concerning the law of the valley."

"I want the people to know I would never endanger their safety. I know why you have the law of only one man leaving the valley at a time and that for hunting. I understand why you do not allow the women and children outside the valley. I honor your law. I also know that my heart says it wants his friends at his marriage. Whatever the council decides, I will understand and respect," Haddok said.

The women brought food and Reed enjoyed the stew. They talked for a while and then Haddok spoke. "I will go and sleep a while. I want to leave the valley before it is light. You can wake me when you have decided."

They agreed and he left the fire to go roll up in some blankets Shining Moon had provided. He was asleep in no time. The safety of the valley engulfed him and he fully understood why they loved the place. He was still in deep sleep when a strong hand shook him awake.

"Haddok. It is time for you to go. It will be light soon," Tall Tree said softly.

Haddok could hardly focus his sleepy eyes. "What did the council decide?"

"We will come to your marriage. The men were happy for us. The decision came easy and quick. We decided to let you sleep as long as possible," Tall Tree said.

"Are you able to make the journey?" Haddok asked.

"Yes. I am getting stronger each day. I can make it."

"If you would agree, I will have two of my men bring horses so you will not have to walk all the way. You know where the last big mountain drops off as you go toward the sunset. I could have them meet you there the day before our marriage."

"That would be good. Tell your men to stop and wait. I will find them."

"I am happy you will come."

"I am happy too. Now come. Let us get you on your way."

Haddok was over the mountain as light began to break. He had a good day of riding to get to Prescott.

10

The sun was leaning far to the west when the three riders entered Prescott. Dust boiled up from the shuffle trot of their horses. It was a hot day. The three men had the look of trouble. Indeed they were.

Dolf Hunter was so big you couldn't miss him. He stood six feet seven inches and weighed a good two hundred eighty pounds. Everything about him was big. He rode a huge black horse, but his size made the horse look small. As big as he was, he was also nimble and amazingly quick with a six gun. His strong suit was his ability to shoot straight. It was said he could hit a jackrabbit in the eye with the rabbit running full speed.

Lize Moffatt was tall and slender. His six feet two inches looked short standing beside Hunter. Moffatt had a wide mean streak and was as good as they come with a pistol.

Wade Morton was a short man stacked like he had been swinging a sledge hammer all his life. In a fist fight, he could probably take the other two easily. He was a moody man with a careless streak in him that would stand him up against anybody. He was also good with his draw.

Ironically the threesome had not planned on riding to Prescott. They had been sitting around a campfire a few days back when the subject of Haddok came up.

"We ain't but about five days away from Prescott," Hunter

said. "What you say we just ride that way and see if anybody has killed Haddok yet."

"Are you saying we ought to kill him if nobody else has?" Morton asked.

"We might as well," Hunter replied.

"They say he's a mighty tough hombre," Moffatt chimed in.

"Well, the last time I heard any news, folks were saying you are a tough hombre Moffatt. Almost as tough as Wade here," Hunter said with a laugh as he nodded toward Morton. "Course nobody thinks I'm tough, but I could hold you boy's horses."

So it was more of a dare than anything else that had pointed them toward Prescott. Any one of them would be a handfull for somebody to stand up to. The three together had trouble hanging all over them.

They tied their horses in front of the Eagle Saloon and walked in. They moved to the bar and ordered a bottle of whiskey. All three downed a glass, washing the trail dust out of their throats.

After a spell, Hunter asked the bartender, "Anybody killed that Haddok feller yet?"

"Nope," he answered. "Why you asking?"

"We been thinking that's a lot of money needing to be spent," Hunter said.

"Well, it may be hard to collect. The word we heard around here is the man named Malone who was handling the offer in Santa Fe for Beecham got hisself killed," the bartender responded.

The three men looked at each other with disappointment in their eyes.

"Did the Beecham feller get killed too?" Morton asked.

"If he did, we ain't heard nothing about it."

"Then I guess the offer still stands," Hunter added.

"I guess it does, if you can find Beecham and collect it," the bartender said. "You might be interested to know Haddok ain't all that easy to kill. There's a bunch of dead folks to prove it."

"That don't bother us none," Hunter replied. He and his partners had not noticed the five men who stood at different times and walked casually out of the saloon.

"How do you get to Haddok's place from here?" Moffatt asked.

"You ride north out of town and follow the wagon ruts. It's about a half day ride," the bartender said.

They finished their bottle and walked to the door. They had talked it over and decided they might as well ride that way and camp for the night. They could go on to his ranch in the morning. When they walked out on the boardwalk they didn't notice the men loitering lazily here and there. It was not until they untied their horses that they noticed the band of about twenty men surrounding them. Each had a rifle or pistol pointing in their direction. That is, all except one.

A short squatty man had a double barreled shotgun leveled on them and the barrels looked as big as stove pipes. Hunter glanced back toward the saloon door, measuring whether or not he could dive back inside. Standing in the door was the bartender. He had a smile on his face and a scattergun in his hands. It was waist high and pointed right at the big man.

Reed Haddok rode into Prescott about the time the men were gathering outside the Eagle saloon. He was down the street at his normal first stop when visiting Prescott. Bob Bussler had been his friend from the first day he set foot in Prescott and the livery was always first on his list. He enjoyed the friendship with Bussler. On this day he put his horse in a stall inside the livery and gave him a scoop of grain. He wondered where Bob might be. He walked out to head for Fort Misery and some supper. He had come to town to invite his friends to his wedding on Saturday and to pick up some special things he wanted to buy for Sam. He also wanted to buy himself some new clothes.

It was not until he walked up to the gathering crowd that he realized something was up. He slipped the loop off his pistol and eased up the boardwalk opposite the saloon. Just at that time the townspeople confronted the three strangers. Nobody knew or noticed his presence. He decided to sit tight and see what was going on.

"What's going on here?" Hunter asked. The three men carefully walked behind their horses and stood in the middle of the circle of men.

"Let me explain it to you," Bob Bussler, the shotgun wielding man, said. "A few of us want to help you understand Prescott ain't no watering hole for people coming to kill Reed Haddok. He probably wouldn't appreciate our help. He likes to handle people like you hisself. But we're helping anyhow. We set store by him around here. I'm gonna read you a page outa his book. We're gonna give you boys a chance to change the direction of your ways. That is, if you want to. If you don't, then this is where you cash in your chips."

"What do you mean?" Moffatt answered.

"You can unbuckle your gunbelts and drop them on the ground. Then you shuck your rifles and do the same. After that, you saddle up and ride as far from Prescott as your horses will carry you," Bussler answered.

"And if we don't," Hunter quizzed, not reading a bit of uncertainty in the eyes of the men facing him.

"Then it's all over for you. We know you came here to kill Haddok. It won't bother us to kill you," Bussler said.

"You boys talk big with all the odds in your favor," Morton said.

"I suppose the three of you against Haddok is what you call fair. The truth is, your odds are probably better pulling iron on us than they are with Haddok. Well, what will it be?" Bussler asked.

The three gunslingers carefully unbuckled their gun belts and let them fall. They then pulled their rifles from their saddle slings and placed them on the ground.

"We might just have to come back and visit you boys again some time," Hunter said as his rifle hit the ground. It was real hard for him to give in.

"Hope you do," Bussler said. "This ain't all of us. I don't think you want to come back here. By the way, by the time your first drink touched your lips a rider was headed to Haddok's ranch. If you decide to change your mind and head that way, you need to know you won't make it. If you head east, south, or west, you've got til sunrise before the ranch hands on the range where you'll be riding will know about you. These men standing with me are off all the ranches around Prescott. Their bosses sent them here and they will be here every day looking for people like you. We aim to serve notice that it ain't one man you'll have to kill. By sun up tomorrow, you'll be fair game for miles and miles around here." Bussler was beginning to like his newfound role in life. He had lied about the rider heading for the Rocking H, but the rest was the truth.

Sensing it all but over, Haddok slipped back toward the livery. He was a little embarrassed and deeply humbled by what he had just seen. He went into the livery and sat down on a grain keg to wait on Bussler.

Meanwhile, the three gunmen stepped into their saddles and rode slowly down the street and out of town heading south. A good way out of town they pulled up and climbed down to fish spare pistols out of their saddle bags.

Standing there humiliated, Moffatt said. "I got the feeling if one of us had sneezed back there we'd all be dead."

"Me too," Morton said.

"What ya'll want to do?" Hunter asked.

Moffatt replied while stepping back into the saddle, "I plan on being as far from this place as I can come sunup."

The other two didn't get to answer him. Moffatt was already riding. They jumped into their saddles and headed out after him.

Bussler was surprised when he found Reed Haddok sitting in the livery when he returned.

"How long you been here?" Bussler asked. He was walking as he talked and he moved over to slap his friend on the shoulder. He was still carrying the shotgun in his left hand.

"Long enough to hear you read them gents from my book," Haddok said with a grin.

"Now listen boy. I didn't want to do that. Everybody else was for it and I'd looked mighty scared if I hadn't a joined in."

"Oh, I know. You was sure acting like you didn't want to. How long ya'll been protecting me?"

"A couple of weeks. All the ranchers came up with the idea and they keep one of their hands here in town all the time. I can't help but notice the fellers they send are pretty fair with a gun," Bussler said with a laugh.

"You don't know how good it makes me feel, Bob. I mean, to have friends like that."

"We all figured it was time this town growed up. It ain't about just you. It's about all of us. I ain't never been as proud of a bunch of people as I am these folks."

"Me too."

"What brings you into town?"

"I'm getting married Saturday. I wanted to tell everybody so the ones who want to come can."

"What about that," Bussler said. "You better put a lot of beans in the pot and cook the biggest steer you got. The whole town will be there."

11

Sam was the prettiest Reed had ever seen her. Her slim full figure shaped the plain white cotton dress her dad hired someone to make. Come to think of it, Reed seldom saw Sam in a dress. She was beautiful. The single white bow holding her black hair looked like a star on a black night. Her eyes were moist and sparkling. The willing smile melted his heart.

Standing beside her and before the preacher had been an apprehensive fear for Reed. He knew it would not be comfortable for him. Yet, here he was and it was easy. He stood looking at Sam and nothing else mattered.

The event was a compromise of sorts. Sam wanted the wedding to take place before he took off looking for Loyd Beecham, even if it meant his father and sister were not there to attend. Reed wanted to get the business with Beecham over with before the wedding so he could forget about him. Sam won out. It suited Reed fine, although he would have loved for his family to be there. Reed wanted a small wedding with just a few people there, but there was no way he could forget his friends.

The ranch yard was covered with wagons and people sitting around fires long before nightfall on Friday. They kept coming on after it was dark. There was music and laughter long into the night. Reed had made sure there was plenty of food for all. He walked among the guests during the evening and enjoyed their company. He was a blessed man to have so many friends. He couldn't help but notice they had a perimeter of defense around the place. These folks were going to make sure he lived long enough to get hog tied.

Reed and Sam spent about three hours during the evening sitting around the table talking with Josh, Raven, Tall Tree, and Shining Moon. He was so happy for Sam and Josh to get to know his Indian friends. Shining Moon had made him a shirt from tanned deer hide and told Reed she had put a special medicine on it that turned away arrows and bullets. Everybody laughed, but Reed caught Shining Moon's eyes and knew she meant it. He hoped it worked. They finally called it a night. Tomorrow would be a big day.

When Reed finally stretched out for the night, he thought, I hope Josh will have the preacher here. He had called Josh off to the side about the middle of the week. "Josh, I'm going to leave it up to you to tell that man I'll give him fifty dollars if he can do a short wedding. The longer he talks, the less he's getting," Reed remembered telling him. Josh laughed when he told him and was still laughing when he returned.

"I thought for a minute he was going to turn you down," Josh had said. "I guess good sense and the fact he hardly ever held fifty dollars in his hand got the best of him and he said he would be here by mid-morning of Saturday."

Morning came and the preacher did show up. Reed found himself standing there saying his vows to Sam. He never saw the tears and pride filling the faces of his friends. Standing beside him were Josh Spencer and Tall Tree. He owed his life to both men. He could go to war with both and never have to worry about his back. They were true friends. Raven stood with Samantha. Their friendship had been sudden and real. Reed couldn't believe it. Even though a host of people stood around them, it was almost like he was in a quiet place with just his friends.

The preacher soon pronounced them married, prayed, and stepped back for Reed to kiss his wife, all in less than twenty minutes. It was a record for the preacher. It was also a disgrace for him to be so short with so many people present to hear him. He managed it however and felt the weight of the silver all the way back to town.

After a long time of hugs, handshakes, and special blessings, the newly wed couple went inside and changed clothes. They came out to horses already saddled and a packhorse laden with supplies waiting for them. They stepped into the saddles and rode away from the ranch, heading for the mountains and stopping at the first high ground to look back on all the commotion at the ranch.

"Where are you taking me?" Sam asked.

"To the valley where me and Josh spent last winter. It's just the place. I cleared it with your father last night. I told him I pegged it as the place while we were up there."

"I didn't know you were thinking about marrying me back then. You had just met me. Why didn't you tell me?" Sam asked.

"Oh, I figured you could read my mind I guess. I ain't surprised you yet," Reed answered.

Sam laughed and said, "I sent Gus Trapp and some of the boys up there day before yesterday to clean it up. I figured that was where you would take me."

"Well, I'll be dog. You are way ahead of me. You scare me just a little Sam. You ain't supposed to be able to read my mind like that," Reed said with his sheepish, quizzical look.

"I know," Sam said. "But you can read mine too. That means we better be careful what we are thinking."

They laughed and headed toward the valley. Reed rode carefully, always aware of Indians and the unexpected appearance of someone wanting to collect the bounty on his head. He had another reason to exercise care now. The magnificent black haired woman who bore his name would never be unguarded.

It was getting late in the day when they rode up to the mountain cabin. They unloaded their gear and Reed built a fire to break the mountain chill in the cabin. After the horses were tended to, Sam put a pot of beans and meat over the fire. They sat in front of the fire and held each other close.

"From the first time I saw you I dreamed that you would be my wife someday," Reed said softly.

"I felt the same way, but I couldn't bear to show it. I thought you were a drifter and would leave as soon as spring came. I hate to admit it, but dad getting shot and all the problems Beecham caused us was really a blessing in a way. It kept you here. Even though I gave you some problems back then, I never really worried after you and Josh showed up at the ranch. There was just something about the two of you. I felt like everything would be okay with you around. I'll admit, I had to grow up a little. My reaction to you going after Beecham was simply that I didn't have any experience at all at being in love," Sam said.

"Me either. I guess we will both have to help each other. I just know you are the most important thing in my life and I have never been happier," Reed said as he pulled her close.

The following three days were like a dream. Reed and Sam enjoyed the powerfully passionate times of giving themselves to each other. There were long periods of time when they enjoyed just talking and sharing their innermost feelings. There were also long periods when they sat silently, holding each other and feeling the energy of their love without words. They walked the valley hand in hand and stopped often for Reed to explain a certain kind of tree or tracks left by an animal. Sam smiled to herself and never let on she knew the sign of every animal in the country and could name every scrub bush or tree. They bathed together in the cold mountain stream. Both voiced how wonderful it would be if they never had to leave the valley.

It was Sam who first brought up the subject of their return to reality.

"Reed, let's get off this mountain and get you headed for Fort Defiance," she said.

"You tired of me already," he shot back with a smile.

"No. I promised you after being so childish the first time you went after Beecham that I wouldn't ever do it again. I don't want you to think I'm going to be hurt every time you say something to me about things that must be done. I know you have to go find him and I'm ready to get it over with," Sam replied.

Reed held her tight for a spell, then said, "We are going to build a strong family. I am so happy to be able to build it with you.

They loaded up their gear and rode down off the mountain, two people in love and with the resolve to do whatever it took to make it.

12

It was well before daylight the next day when Haddok walked out with Sam to head for Fort Defiance. Josh and Raven, along with Tall Tree and Shining Moon, were standing by his horse. His Indian friends were going to leave for their village later in the day. They had waited for Reed and Sam to return. Tall Tree had offered to ride with Reed. Reed turned him down without hurting his feelings. Josh had been adamant about going along. Reed didn't worry about hurting his feelings. He simply told his friend the one thing he could do for him that really mattered was to protect the ranch and his wife. Josh didn't like it, but he knew Reed better than all the rest. He was a tougher warrior when alone. He told his friend not to worry about anything with them.

Haddok hugged and kissed his wife, thanked his friends again, and stepped into the saddle. He would be trailing one pack horse. Elsbie Cotton, a lanky cowhand, who could hold his own about anywhere, was holding Haddok's horses. As Haddok took the reins and started walking the horses out of the yard, Cotton walked along beside him til until they were out of earshot of the others.

"Boss, I'd be mighty proud to ride along with you," Cotton said.

"Thanks friend. I know you'd do it and it makes me feel good. But you need to stay here and help take care of this place."

"I thought I might tell you something you'd get a kick out of before you left. Josh sent me and Simmons out to meet your Indian friends before the wedding. He told us where to go and then to wait til they found us. We went right where he said and kinda pulled back in the brush a bit to keep outta sight. We'd been there about three hours and we were talking low like so nobody could hear us. Then the strangest thing happened. I swear to God we was just settin' there jawing back and forth with one another and all of a sudden that big Indian friend of yours was settin' right there between us. Scared the plain devil out of me and Simmons both. He smiled real big and said he was your friend. After we got him and his wife on the horses and started back, me and Simmons got so tickled we nearly fell off our horses. Now, I've faced some pretty tough fellers in my lifetime and ain't of a notion to get jumpy. I'm telling you I was plain scared. I hadn't felt like that since I jumped into a nest of water snakes when I was a kid."

Haddok was laughing out loud as he listened to Elsbie. When he stopped talking, Haddok said, "You ain't the only one he ever done that way. His people named him He Who Runs With Spirits. They shortened it to Ghost Runner. Believe me, he deserves the name."

"Well, I figured you might get a little bored on this trip and it might do you good while settin' by them fires alone just to think about these two big tough cowhands shaking like a dog crappin' peach seeds." Cotton was laughing with him now.

The two clasped hands and Haddok turned and rode out of the yard.

Reed had talked to some people while in town before the wedding who had traveled the way he was going and he had a general route in his mind. When it started getting light he shifted into his caution mode and rode light in the saddle. When he could get his bearings he headed due east and headed toward the mountains. By mid-day he was in the valley stretched out below the Mogollon rim. He turned northeast and camped the first night below the rim.

He knew he was in Apache country and he had no desire to have a run in with them. He camped dry and careful. He weathered the night rolled up in two blankets. He was hunkered down in the thickest brush he could find. He felt like a rabbit during the night and a fool come daylight. He was kicking himself about not having a fire. He would have wrestled a mountain lion for a cup of coffee by the time he stepped into the saddle.

He rode up as close to the base of the sheer face of the rim and followed it until he came up on a well used trail. It was covered with unshod horse tracks. It made him more cautious. He followed the trail through a number of switchbacks, riding slow and alert. He didn't want to get caught halfway up by a bunch of Apaches coming down. He topped out into some of the finest timber he had ever seen. The pines were so tall he got a little woozy tilting his head and looking at their swaying tops. They grew thick. There was not much underbrush. The big trees shielded the sunlight so not much would grow under them.

This was dangerous country. You could ride right up on somebody if you didn't stop often to look and listen. He had an idea about how long it would take him to get to Fort Defiance. At this speed it might take me a month, he thought.

He continued his northeast track and was still in the big woods at nightfall. He hunkered down in a small hollow and spent another night without a fire. He took some grain out of his pack and fed the horses. He watered them out of his water bag and tied them so they could move around a little. He had them in real close. They were the best thing he had going for him when it came to letting him know if somebody was coming. He rolled up in his blankets and thought about Sam and then the job he had to do at Fort Defiance. Somewhere along the way the long day in the saddle got the best of him and he dozed off. He was easily back into his pattern of sleeping a little and then waking up to listen to the night sounds. It was how he stayed alive while alone on the trail. He felt no warning during the night and saddled up and rode out at daybreak with a piece of jerked beef in his mouth.

About the middle of the afternoon he pulled up on a high

point looking out over a vast valley of timber sporting a scattering of grassy meadows here and there. He spotted some movement in one of the meadows directly to his front. He fished out his eyeglass and focused on the meadow. It was a bunch of deer. He counted ten. They were grazing on the grass and moving slowly away from him. The wind was to his back. He figured it was cool enough the thermal was not pushing his scent down on them. He felt good about seeing them relaxed. If anybody was between him and the meadow they would surely be moving fast out of there. He made up his mind to steer clear of the meadows. He didn't want to spend any time in the open and he certainly didn't want to leave a trampled trail.

His third night was another dry camp. He found another low area shielded by the terrain around him and bedded down for a good night's sleep. Daybreak found him already saddled and riding. Moving slowly and very watchful, he thought, I've been riding three days and I havent seen a single soul, white or Indian. He knew full well that didn't mean they hadn't seen him. He stopped often to check his back trail and what lay before him. He couldn't see far enough to do much good with either.

By the sun, it was on into the afternoon when he came up on Morman lake. It was a large body of water and had been the first major landmark the folks back in Prescott told him to look out for. He stayed back from the lake and moved around it until he was a little north of it. It was getting dark when he made camp. The first thing he did was build a fire. He knew it was a risk but he wanted some fried meat and coffee. He built it of dry wood that gave off very little smoke. By the time it got good and dark the fire was down to coals. He set the skillet full of sliced cured meat and the coffee pot on the coals. He enjoyed his first hot meal in three days, washing down the meat with boiling hot coffee. He cleaned up the skillet and put it back in the pack. Pouring himself another cup of coffee, he leaned back against his saddle and relaxed. When he finished his second cup of coffee he removed Reuben Partlow's rifle from the packhorse frame and cleaned it good. He brought it along for a purpose. If he needed to do some distance shooting, the long barreled fifty caliber was the very thing. He had taken time to shoot the rifle and get used to it before he left. It was a powerful weapon with amazing accuracy. He couldn't help but think about how a man planned to kill him with it. When he finished, he poured another cup of coffee

13

Reed was just finishing his coffee and was about to go get him another cup when he noticed both horses raise their heads abruptly and look off toward the lake. He spoke softly to them to calm them down. Their eyes were locked on whatever was out there and did not let up. He put his cup down, eased his rifle up and rolled over to crawl back into the darkness away from the fire. He waited, listening for any telltale movement or sound that might give away what was out there. He heard nothing. The horses seemed more relaxed now. He was about to give up and go for the coffee cup when he heard a voice float out of the darkness.

"We smelled your coffee and we ain't had none in a few days. We'd be obliged if you would spare us a cup."

Reed was quiet for a minute and then spoke. "How many traveling with you?" He moved about ten feet to the left.

"Just two of us. I'm Rebel Tanner and my buddy is Dub Lawson. We're out of Texas heading for the gold country," the man replied.

"You bringing any trouble?"

"No siree. The only trouble we got is we're out of coffee," Tanner said.

"Ride on in then. I've got coffee to spare and I know what it's like to be without," Haddok said. He moved again to his left.

Reed watched as they rode up to about fifteen feet from the fire and dismounted. They were leading one pack horse. He was relieved to see there was not one sign about them that they were gunfighters. The first thing they did was fish out their coffee cups and head for the pot. Reed walked into the light, rifle held casually in their direction, and motioned for them to go ahead and help themselves. He found his cup and carefully, without taking his eyes off them, poured himself another cup. They sat down across the coals of the fire and savored the coffee like it was a warm woman on a cold night.

After a spell, one of them spoke. "Feller, this here is the best coffee ever I had. Scuse the bad manners. I'm Rebel Tanner. This here is Dub Lawson."

Reed nodded without reaching across with his hand to shake and did not give them his name. That wasn't unusual. A lot of people never volunteered their name right off. It didn't bother them right then. The coffee had their attention.

"Where you headed?" Reed asked.

"We've been punching cows most our lives. We decided to try our luck at finding us some gold. There's a lot of talk back in Texas about people striking it rich in Colorado. We decided to give it a turn," Turner said. Lawson hadn't said a word.

"What part of Texas you from?"

"The up to now silent Lawson said, "We're from the country around Abilene. Ever been there?"

"Nope. I hear it's good cattle country," Haddok answered. "I hope you gents have some luck with the gold."

The two strangers looked at each other and Lawson kind of jabbed Tanner in a kidding way and said, "We thought we might drift by Prescott and collect the money on that Haddok feller's head and use it for our grubstake. We hear ain't nobody claimed it yet." They both laughed.

Haddok grinned a mite and said, "I hear he's still alive. It might be a quick way for you to get some money."

"He must be a prize bronc. The talk back home is that ain't nobody been able to saddle him yet," Lawson said.

They both motioned as if asking if they could have some more coffee. Haddok nodded his approval and they were reaching for the pot when Tanner asked, "We didn't get your name. What would it be?"

"The name's Haddok," Reed said with a smile, as he stood up.

They both stopped with cups in mid-air as they slowly got up.

"Now listen here, Mr. Haddok. We was just joshin around," Tanner said. "Ole Dub here is always runnin off at the mouth and it usually gets us in trouble. Why ain't neither one of us worth a cuss in a gun fight and the last thing we want is trouble with you."

Lawson was nodding in agreement like a deacon on the amen bench.

Haddok smiled. "Don't worry. If I'd sized you up as trouble, you wouldn't be at my fire drinking my coffee. The only thing I'm worried about with you being here is I don't ever know when trouble is going to show up. You boys could be here when it comes and I'd sure hate for you to get caught up in it." Haddok chuckled to himself as he talked, already aware they were anxious to ride out of there by the way they were shaking the coffee out of their cups.

"What you saying?" Lawson asked.

"I'd sure hate for you innocent boys to be here and share my grief when some of these fellows who want me dead show up."

"You ain't got to worry about that Mr. Haddok," Tanner said. Both men were a good bit older than Reed and their use of the word mister brought another inner chuckle. "We're going to ride and you don't have to worry about us telling anybody where you are." Both men were keeping their hands so far from their pistols they looked awkward.

"Well, ya'll be careful out there in the dark. You'll be riding through some Apache country and I'd sure hate for you to stumble up on a bunch of them. I'll probably be riding behind you come daylight." Haddok knew they had no idea of the route he was taking and he didn't think it would hurt for them to think he was headed the same way they were. It might help them move on a mite just in case twenty thousand dollars got to looking big to them after they got away from his camp.

They thanked him again for the coffee and lit out, moving a lot faster than he would want to ride at night. He smiled to himself as he poured another cup of coffee and thought, I hope them pilgrims don't ride off some bluff.

Haddok woke the next morning to a light drizzle. There were enough hot coals left in his fire to nurse it back to life. He made some coffee and hunkered under his slicker and enjoyed it as enough light showed up to allow things to take shape around him. He packed up, stepped into the saddle and rode out, continuing toward the northeast.

He rode in the light rain through the day and stopped when he found a thick deadfall of an old tree still covered with leaves. It was pretty dry under it and he settled in for a night of sporadic cold rain drops working their way through the thick cover to splatter on his slicker. The ground cloth and slicker kept him dry, but it was a miserable night.

Morning brought a clear day and it felt good to ride in the sunshine. Late in the day he came up to what he believed was the Little Colorado River. The folks back in Prescott had told him it would be the first good sized stream he'd come to after leaving Morman Lake. The river ran pretty much north and south at that point and he was looking for a smaller tributary coming in from due east. On a hunch he headed south and a few miles downstream he found it. He forded the river and spent the night back in the brush from the mouth of the smaller stream.

He spent the next two days following the smaller stream. He held back away from it just in case there were Indians or others traveling the banks. About mid-day of the first day the small stream split and he chose to follow the northernmost finger. The flow of water became smaller as he began to climb and seemed to play out when he topped out on a plateau. It was a beautiful grassland. The grass was belly high on his horse. He didn't like being out in the open. He traveled slowly and glassed the area in front of him often. He didn't want to ride up on trouble.

He rode carefully for three days. He could have made better time, but he spotted two villages ahead of him. He figured them to be Navajo. Both villages made him swing a wide loop. He didn't want any Indian trouble if he could help it. He saw their herds and some riders watching them. He had never had dealing with them so his best bet was to avoid them.

About the middle of the third day later, he glassed a herd of cattle being moved by some cowhands. He rode toward them and pulled up as a couple of the men rode out to meet him.

"Howdy," Haddok said. "I'm traveling a new trail and I'm trying to get to Fort Defiance. Am I anywhere close to finding it?"

"You're headed right," one of the men said. "It's about forty miles due east. Matter of fact, if you follow the tracks of our herd you'll come close. We brought these cows out of a valley about three miles from Fort Defiance."

"Thanks. I appreciate your help," Haddok said as he rode away from the men.

He rode the rest of the day and the next formulating his plan of how he would begin his search for Beecham once he got there.

14

Haddok followed the cattle tracks and pushed hard trying to cover the forty miles as fast as he could. He came up to where the cattle came out of the valley. He knew he was close. He looked around and found a ridge covered with small trees and brush. It was thick. He rode that way and found a small animal trail leading into it. He followed the trail to the highest spot and dismounted. He took a little time to clear out a place big enough for the horses, a fire, and room to stretch out and sleep. He gathered some dead wood in the fading light and settled in to what would be home for a spell. He planned to be as unnoticed as possible in Fort Defiance. He would come back to his camp and sleep at night. He would leave the pack horse here. He hoped he would be seen as a local puncher and not attract any attention.

Come daylight, after a bait of coffee, he rode back out the same small trail and headed toward Fort Defiance. There was a military garrison stationed there to protect the settlers headed west. A large settlement, as usual, had sprung up around the fort. His first glance at the town told him it was a thriving community.

He rode slowly down the street, giving the appearance he was in no hurry with nothing on his mind. Traveling men always attracted the attention of town folk and the last thing he wanted was attention. He tied up at a rail outside the building that had the word café burned onto a board hanging above the door. He walked in, sat down, and ordered himself some steak and eggs. He sat quietly and ate his meal. He was all ears. He knew Loyd Beecham had ordered a message to be sent to a man named Frank Lain. It was to be picked up from the stage office.

He was seated at a table in the corner. He sized up the crowd as he ate. He took his time and listened to the small talk. He didn't learn a thing. He felt good about the fact that nobody seemed to pay him any attention. When he finished, he paid up and left. It was time to find the stage office.

It was on the north edge of town. He walked in as the only man in the room worked on some papers while sitting at a small desk in the corner. The man looked up and asked, "Can I help you?"

"Maybe," Haddok answered. He walked over and extended his hand to the man. "My name's Reed. I was hoping you could give me a little information."

"Howdy," the man replied with a pleasant voice. "What kind of information you looking for?"

"I'm headed west to hook up with my outfit in the Colorado territory. I bought some cattle back east and they are driving them on ahead of me. I came by this way because I'm looking for a man who owes me some money from a land deal a spell back. His name is Frank Lain. He cut out without paying me and a friend of his said he thought he was headed here. Do you know him?"

The man looked a little puzzled and said, "No sir. I don't know him. However, I've heard of him. There's a gent who has come in here every four or five days over the last six weeks asking if a letter has come addressed to Frank Lain. There ain't been no letter. I asked the man if I could get it to him when it came and he told me he'd just keep checking back."

"If you don't mind me asking, what did the feller look like?"

"He's a tall man. He has the looks of a cowhand. I followed him outside one day and got a look at the brand on his horse. Didn't recognize it. He ain't from a ranch around here."

"Which way does he head out of town when he leaves?"

"He always heads north out of town. I've watched him leave

a couple of times. I thought it was a little strange he wouldn't tell me anything about where I could find him."

"I'd appreciate it if you keep our conversation between us. If I find him and collect my money, I'll make it worth your while."

"Oh, that ain't necessary. I'll keep it quiet."

"You say he comes in every few days. How long has it been since he's been here?"

"It's been a spell. Probably about time for him to show up again if he keeps up his pace. Are you staying some place in town? I could get word to you when he comes."

"I ain't staying in town, But I'll be here every day for a while. I might hang around here pretty close if it don't bother you. I won't cause no trouble."

"It won't bother me. You make yourself at home. Maybe you'll get lucky."

"I sure do appreciate it. I didn't get your name when I came in."

"I'm sorry. It's Rafe Spooner."

"Well Rafe, it's good to meet you." Haddok reached out to shake his hand again, thanked him for his time, and then walked outside. He led his horse across the street to the livery and asked the hostler to give him a bait of grain. He also asked him to sack him up about twenty-five pounds of grain to take with him later. He walked out and found himself a shade at the corner of the livery. He sat down to relax. He had a clear view of the stage office. Anybody looking him over would have thought he was asleep, the way he was sloped down with his hat over his eyes. It wasn't so. He was wide awake and observing everything he could out on the street.

Late in the afternoon he walked back to the café, ate supper, and returned to get his horse. As he rode out he went close to the stage office and waved at Spooner. It had been a good day. He now knew somebody was checking for the letter to Beecham. All he had to do was hang close to the stage office for a few days and get lucky. It was dark when he rode into his camp. He built a fire to break the chill, fed his pack horse some grain, put the coffee on and settled in to get some rest.

The next two days were spent in almost the same manner. He would arrive in Fort Defiance early and hung close to the stage office except when he walked down to the café to eat. He avoided conversations with people and maintained a constant vigilance on the entrance to the stage office. A lot of people went in and out of the office but none brought a signal from Spooner.

It was getting on into the morning of the fourth day when Haddok noticed a lanky cowhand tie up in front of the saloon next to the stage office. The man went inside. Haddok's intuition told him to stay put. About a half hour later the cowhand came out and walked next door to the stage office. He went in and stayed only a minute before he came back out and went to his horse. Spooner came outside and motioned toward the man with his thumb and nodded to Haddok. Reed nodded back and stood, walking quickly to get his horse.

Haddok stepped into the saddle and casually walked his horse out of town ahead of the man. He looked as if he was going nowhere in a hurry. When out of town, he pulled off the road as if he was going east. He got far enough away from the road to hide himself and watched as the cowhand rode by along the road. Reed watched until the man was out of sight over the first rise. He then kicked his horse into a trot and pulled up to look over the rise. He saw the man ride out of sight around a curve.

Reed pulled off the road and went down into the low land where he found some open terrain. He pushed his horse into a full run and rode about twenty minutes before he turned back west. He soon came up to the road and turned south as if he was headed for Fort Defiance. He walked his horse and acted as if he had no interest other than finding the town.

A few minutes later he rounded a bend and saw the cowhand riding toward him. They met as naturally as two travelers going in opposite direction could.

"Howdy," Haddok said as he lifted his hand and pulled up facing the man. "The name's Reed. I'm headed for Fort Defiance. Will this track get me there?"

"Yep," the man replied. "You are no more than an hour out."

"Thanks. I'm looking for work. Do you know of any outfits around here who may be hiring?"

"Nope. I work on out at Two Buttes Ranch. Our boss ain't looking for any help. I don't know much about the other outfits around here. I ain't from here so I can't help you much."

"Two Buttes. Never heard of it from the gents I've talked to on the trail. Is it a big outfit?"

"Not really. We run about three hundred head. That's about all the boss wants."

"Where is it?" Reed asked casually. He acted like he really didn't want to know.

"Oh, I'm about three hours away."

"Well, thanks anyway. Keep your saddle under you," Reed said as he lifted his hand again and nudged his horse on. He didn't look back. As he rode, he thought, I've got the place. Two Buttes Ranch. I guess I'll have to pull up camp and move a little north.

15

Haddok broke camp soon after daybreak the next morning and headed northeast. He planned to ride around Fort Defiance and hit the road north out of town. He headed up to the road and sat back from it a spell. He didn't want anybody seeing him. There was no sign of any travelers so he eased out and went north.

He remembered the cowhand from the Two Buttes ranch saying he was about three hours away from the ranch. He could travel along the road for about two hours and then find the right place to hole up. He would be just about right to look around a while and check out the ranch. As the road dwindled down to nothing more than wagon ruts, Haddok figured he was getting close.

He left the road on a rocky brush covered ridge and made his way west until he got into some timber. About thirty minutes later he found what he was looking for. A rock shelf about twenty feet high ran around the north side of a mountain. An old animal trail ran below the shelf. He took it and came up on a overhang reaching about twenty-five feet back into the mountain. He set up camp there.

He spent the rest of the day getting settled in and checking out the area. His camp could not be seen from above and the only easy access to it was the small trail he took coming in. Anybody coming up the mountain toward him would have a tough time. It was too steep to come straight up and they would have to make a lot of racket.

He found a faint trail that switched back and forth leading to the bottom. He decided he would try it the next morning when he went to find the ranch. He built a fire a little before dark and cooked some bacon and beans. He ate his fill along with a pot of coffee. He then settled in for the night.

It was getting on to light when he led his horse down the mountain the next morning. The trail worked fine. He stopped when he was down and looked back to mark the trail in his mind. It always looked different from the opposite direction and he didn't want to make a wrong turn on his way back.

He then mounted up and rode carefully through the timber in the bottom until it played out. He sat his horse looking out over rolling grassland that offered very little cover. He took his eyeglass and scanned the area. His attention rested on two gigantic peaks that looked like somebody had sliced the tops off them. He thought, so these are the two buttes the ranch is named for. They stood above the grassland like giants. They lay due north of his position.

He studied the terrain, looking for some avenue of approach that would conceal his presence. Seeing none, he decided to ride back inside the tree line and follow it as it seemed to bend back north. It could be that he would be able to see the ranch from up ahead of the bend. The trees continued up over a knoll that rose up to his left front. He topped the knoll in the trees. He slipped to the edge and spotted another knoll about a quarter of a mile away. The bend in the tree line continued, so he slipped back into the woods and followed it. When he reached the top of the next knoll the land dropped off in front of him toward the buttes. There were successive rolls in the land between him and the buttes. He couldn't see what was in the depression between the high places but he had a good view of the base of the buttes. His eyes caught something shiny at the foot of the one closest to him and he glassed it to see a series of buildings. Smoke was trickling up from the chimney of one. He had found the ranch.

He rode back into the woods and tied his horse. He scouted

out a place where he could lie down and study the ranch with his eyeglass. He figured it was at least a mile or more to the buildings from his position. He couldn't make out much. He scoped the area thoroughly, looking for some way he could get in unnoticed. It looked impossible.

The ranch was built with defense in mind. You couldn't approach it without being seen. The only dead spot was from directly behind the buildings. That was no option because the butte was a steep drop and Haddok had no intention of dying in that manner. From all indications, a few men could hold off an army from the ranch.

Haddok thought over the situation. He had hoped to get close enough to see how many men Beecham had around him. He knew Beecham's style. He would hire guns to hide behind. Haddok thought, he sure picked the right place to hole up. The man was shrewd. Haddok's plan had been to get close enough to Beecham to whittle down the odds a bit. It didn't appear his plan would work. The only other thing he knew to do was to get Beecham's hired guns to come to him. He thought, I've got to think this thing out.

Haddok stayed a little longer and then left for his camp. He would spend the night there and sort through his options. He planned on going back into Fort Defiance tomorrow.

16

Haddok arrived at Fort Defiance around noon the next day. He left both horses at the livery, he walked down the street to the Blanton Hotel, and rented a room. He brought his gear up to the room before finding a place to get a bath and shave. Clean and revived, he went to the café and had a good meal. The crowd there was quiet. He had been in town enough to arouse no attention by his presence. Nobody seemed to care anyway.

His plan to get Beecham was now set in his mind. It was a simple plan. Anybody coming off the ranch would not go back. Sooner or later Beecham would run out of gunslingers to protect him. He would then have to make a run for it. Haddok never considered that Beecham would personally come looking for him. He knew him too well. He couldn't bring himself to believe Beecham wanted to see him.

He finished his meal and walked down the street to a building where a sign out front said Sheriff's Office. He ambled in to meet the man with the badge.

"Sheriff," Reed said, "I need to talk to you. My name is Reed Haddok."

The sheriff stood with a look of surprise. "I'm Eli Bowles. Everybody in the country has heard about you. I never figured to meet you. What in the world are you doing in Fort Defiance?"

"I'm on the trail of Loyd Beecham," Reed said.

"I've heard about him too. He's the fellow who put the price on your head, ain't he?"

"Yep. He's a ruthless man. He's left a lot of dead men on his back trail. I ran him off from Arizona and he's been sending people to try and kill me ever since. I've tracked him here and I believe he's holed up at a place north of here called the Two Buttes ranch."

"Well, what about that. It kind of explains some things for me. There have been at least five gunslinger types who have come through town the last few weeks asking directions to the Two Buttes. You may be right," the sheriff said.

"I'm sure he ain't using the name Beecham. The word I got was he might be using the name he hid under in Santa Fe. He was known as Frank Lain there."

"He ain't used either one here. A man by the name of Lansford bought the place a couple of years back. Jake Lansford I believe it was. I've never met him. The banker told me about the deal right after it happened. Old Pete Dawson owned the place up til then. He was a fine old man who just got too old to hang on. He sold the place and moved back east somewhere. The banker said this man Lansford was a curious sort. Seemed like he didn't want anybody to know he had bought the place. Said he had some family problems and didn't want his kin catching up to him."

"Do you think the banker would talk to me about Lansford? It might make me sure I'm on the right trail."

"He would if he was here. He left about a year ago."

"Did anybody else you know of meet Lansford?"

"Nope. Everybody in town thought it was strange. He bought the place and hadn't been seen or heard of since. Some of the hands come to town every now and then, but they are shut mouthed about the ranch. None of the men I've seen from out there appear to be the sort to take care of a working ranch."

"Well, I'm betting Lansford is really my man Beecham. I figure he bought the place as a nest for him to hide out when he needed it. He has that kind of money. I got word he had left Santa Fe and headed here."

"What do you plan to do?" the sheriff asked.

"I've scouted the ranch out and it would be tough for me to get to him the way it's laid out. Your talk about the gunslingers coming through town makes me even more sure. That's how he operates. He hires guns to protect him. What I aim to do is cut the protection down and flush him out. That's why I'm here. I don't plan to bring any trouble into your town if I can help it. I may not be able to avoid it once they learn I'm here. I didn't want you to think I'm some kind of trouble maker. The truth is, if Beecham is at the Two Buttes ranch and I don't get him, you'll have to deal with him sooner or later. He's the type who will do whatever it takes to get what he wants. The law don't make any difference with him. He'd just as soon have you killed as me."

"I'm glad you've let me in on what you're doing. Word came through here last week that the man in Santa Fe who did Beecham's talking for the bounty on your head was found dead. Did you kill him?"

"No. I came here straight from Prescott. I've been busy dealing with the people Beecham sent to kill me."

"What can I do to help you?" the sheriff asked.

"Nothing. I can handle it. I just didn't want to start the dance before I talked to you. Some people on his payroll will get killed. I want you to know I stand for law and order. This is one of them things where a man just has to do what he's got to do."

"I understand. I've been pulling for you all along. Seems like everybody has. You've got a good name with everybody I know."

"That makes me feel good. You've got to understand I never planned for any of this to happen. I did what I thought was right back there and Beecham has been after me ever since. I'm going to put an end to it. I'd appreciate it if you keep our conversation private until I get ready to let him know I'm here."

"You've got it, and anything else I can do to help. I'm afraid I can't offer much gun help."

"That won't be necessary. Like I said earlier, I'm going to try and take care of this business away from town. If trouble shows up here, don't feel like it's your place to get involved. He'll have the best gunmen money can buy around him and they can chew up and spit out most lawmen. I'm not questioning your ability with a gun. They won't face you one on one. They pile up against you and it's like signing your death warrant to face them. They are ruthless and will shoot you in the back if they get the chance. That's the main reason I don't want anybody fighting my battles."

"Well, I ain't afraid to die. I wear this badge for a reason. When the time comes I can't handle it, I'll hang it up."

"I know that. Don't think I'm trying to make a small town lawman out of you. It's just easier for me to handle it myself."

"Do you think you can do it, son?" the sheriff asked in a fatherly voice.

"Yes sir, I sure do. It won't be pretty, but I'll get her done," Reed said.

They talked on briefly and then shook hands before Haddok left. He headed for the hotel to get some sleep. His work was about to pick up. After he left, the sheriff thought, I can see now why everybody who knows the boy likes him.

17

Haddok slept well and woke up to a quiet morning. He went to the window and peered out. The street was clear except for a few horses tied to hitching rails here and there. A dog barked a few times and a rooster crowed somewhere behind the hotel. He dressed and made his way to the café for breakfast. He enjoyed the quiet morning. Only a handful of people were eating when he took his seat at the window table. Some of those had left by the time his food arrived.

His thoughts, as always, went to Sam. He hoped she was handling his absence better than he was. He knew he was a lucky man to have a woman like her to love him. He thought, man, it still sounds a little strange to realize she is my wife.

He whiled away the food thinking of their few days of happiness in the beautiful mountain valley. He had relived those days often since he left for Fort Defiance. He was nudged back to reality by movement outside catching his eyes.

Two men were hitching their horses to the rail in front of the saloon across the street from him. One of them was the cowhand from the Two Buttes ranch he had talked to on the trail. This is my lucky day, Reed thought. It's time to start the dance. His plan was to hold the cards until he had the right opportunity to stir the pot at the Two Buttes ranch. These gents being in town gave him the opportunity.

The first thing he needed to know was how many gunslingers

Beecham had protecting him out at the ranch. It was hard for Haddok to wait. He had forced himself to stay off the ranch until he was ready. It had paid off. He now had his eyes on two cowhands off the ranch who could provide him with the information. He would be waiting on them down the road when they began their return trip.

Haddok paid for his breakfast and went to saddle his horse and load his pack horse at the livery. He hitched the horses in front of the hotel and took a seat in the shade along the boardwalk. He leaned back, shaded his eyes with his hat, and looked the part of a sleepy morning in Fort Defiance. In spite of the look, his senses were running full out. Loyd Beecham had made life uncertain for him with the bounty on his head. Haddok had kicked himself plenty for letting Beecham walk when he was a beaten man. Should have ended it then and there, he thought. When he had those thoughts, the man he was always came to the top and said, you did the right thing. At the moment he was thinking he could be home with his wife if he had ended it then. One thing he knew for certain. It would end soon. Up to now, his presence was unknown by everyone at the ranch. By the end of the day, Beecham and his men would know. Haddok breathed deep and enjoyed the moment of peace. It might be the last he would have for a spell.

Ross and Cliff Partain walked out of the saloon about mid-morning. They stood looking up and down the street. They walked over toward the café, passing right in front of Haddok. Haddok watched their feet as they went by and looked up to see them enter the café.

Reed stepped down from the walk, unhitched his horses, hoisted himself into the saddle, and casually rode up the street and out of town heading north. After about a half hour ride he found the spot he liked to wait on the two riders. It was along a straight stretch of the road running through some timber. He tied the horses well back in the trees. He then walked to the side of the road and set down to wait.

His wait lasted about an hour. He heard them a good five

minutes before he saw them. They were walking their horses and talking a mile a minute. They were completely surprised when Haddok stepped out from behind a tree, pistol in hand. They pulled up in shock, staring down the barrel of his pistol.

"What you want from us, feller? We ain't got no money," Ross Partain said.

"Get down off your horses and walk over here," Haddok ordered. "Be real careful. How you act the next few minutes might decide whether you're alive or dead come sundown." He pointed in the direction he wanted them to walk and they did exactly what he said.

"Who are you? Why you got it in for us?" Cliff asked with a worried look.

"Hey! I've seen you before ain't I," Ross asked. "I met you on the road a few days back. You was looking for work."

Reed smiled. "I've found me some work. Now all I got to do is decide whether or not you are a part of it."

The Partain brothers looked at each other, not understanding what he was talking about or where he was headed with all this.

"Are you gents headed back to the Two Buttes ranch?" Haddok asked.

"Yep. That is if you'll let us," Ross replied. Both men were wearing pistols. Neither had even hinted at moving a hand in that direction.

"Well, I need some information about what's going on out there and I need a message delivered to whoever is running the show," Haddok replied.

"We've been working there for a spell, but there ain't been much work going on," Ross said.

"How'd you boys get tied up with the Two Buttes?" Reed asked. His hand held his pistol casually in their direction.

"A man by the name of Lansford bought the place a while back and hired seven of us men to look after the place. He left and was gone over a year and a half. He showed back up about two months ago. He's running ahead of some trouble and he's hiring gunfighters as fast as he can. He asked me and Cliff to help protect him. We've about decided to ride. Are you the feller he's running from?" Ross asked.

"I guess I am," Haddok answered. "My name is Reed Haddok and the man you're working for is Loyd Beecham."

All the blood drained from the faces of the Partain brothers. They glanced at each other with the countenance of egg sucking dogs. "I guess everybody in the country has heard about you and Beecham. You got to believe me when I say we ain't got a dog in this fight. If you'll let us, we'll ride and you won't see us again," Ross said.

"I ain't ever killed nobody I haven't had to. If you and anybody else at the Two Butte rides out by tomorrow, there will be no trouble from me. If I ever see you again, there will be no talking. It'll be up to you to steer clear of me."

"That's fair enough," Cliff said. "We'll ride."

"I want you to deliver a message to Beecham. I also want to know how many gunmen he's hired. I'd like to know their names."

"We'll take your message. As for the gunslingers, he's had seven to show up so far. They rode in from Kansas. Two of them are men we know about. One is Burl Isom and the other is Wiley Pounds. They both have killed a lot of men in their day. Beecham keeps us separated from them. Their job is to protect him and kill you. At least that's what we have overheard. We don't know any of the others," Ross said.

"Fine. This is the message I want you to give to Beecham and his men. Anybody who rides off the Two Butte by sundown tomorrow, and keeps riding, is free to go. Beecham is the only one that can't leave. Tell them I've got plenty of time and I'll whittle the stick down til ain't nobody left but him. After sundown tomorrow, nobody leaves that ain't dead. Can you remember all that?" Haddok asked.

"We sure can," Ross replied.

Without another word, Reed walked to his horse, stepped into the saddle, and rode off, never taking his eyes off the two men.

When he was out of sight, Ross turned to his brother and said, "You had this game pegged Cliff. What do you think? Do we ride now, or go take the message and then ride?"

"I want to ride now. But Haddok might be watching us and I'd hate to run now and have him stop us. Let's take the message and then ride."

"What if Beecham won't let us leave?"

"I say we keep that to ourselves and ride out tonight. We won't even talk about leaving."

"Sounds good to me. Cliff, did you notice how cool that man is? It made me nervous being around him. I'm thinking I know why Beecham is such a scared man and I think he's got a good reason for it." They saddled up and rode toward the ranch.

18

Haddok headed immediately for the camp he had made earlier and left the pack horse there. Before leaving, he took Partlow's rifle out of the pack and grabbed a fistful of fifty caliber rounds. He then wound his way down from his camp and rode to the place where he had observed the Two Butte ranch on his first trip out. He left his horse well back from the tree line and walked to the spot where he had glassed the ranch buildings. He had the big rifle and his eyeglass with him as he carefully moved around to find the perfect place.

He found some high ground allowing him a good view of the buildings. He settled into the prone position back into the bushes. He didn't want the muzzle flash or smoke to give his position away. He focused the eyeglass and studied the layout. The rolling hills between his position and the ranch buildings made it hard to estimate the range. He knew the bullet would drop a good deal from where he was. He would have to allow for it.

At that moment, he noticed some movement around the ranch. People were walking around. He couldn't make out any of them. One might be Beecham, he thought. He was tempted to let one fly, but he wanted to wait. He wanted the Partain boys to tell it all before he began to spook them.

He took the big rifle and unfolded the two prongs serving as support at the end of the barrel. He put the stock to his shoulder and sighted down the barrel. He flipped the rear sight up and rolled it all the way down to the bottom. He knew it was probably a greater distance than the range of the sight. Satisfied, he slipped a round in the breach and locked it. He then picked the eyeglass back up and waited.

19

The Partain brothers went through the gate at the Two Buttes ranch about twenty minutes after Haddok had settled into his position watching the ranch. They rode slowly up to the main building and yelled for everybody to come out.

Beecham was the first, followed by Harper and Walls. Melton and Horton came from behind the house and they were joined by Isom, Pounds, and Garron who came up from the bunk house. Three of the other men joined them.

"What's up?" Beecham asked.

"Well, we were stopped by a gent on the way back to the ranch. He sent us to tote a message for him. He said his name was Haddok," Ross Partain said.

"Where was he?" Beecham asked nervously, looking back down the road.

"We were about an hour out of Fort Defiance when he stopped us. He was a good two hours ride from here," Ross added.

"What did he look like?" Beecham asked.

"He looked about twenty years old on a six three frame that appeared to be all muscle. He was cool as a winter breeze and didn't show us much regard. He never pointed his pistol right at us. He held it like a toy. We both got the idea he knew how to handle it. He was all business," the older Partain said.

"What was his message?" Garron asked.

"He told us who he was and then he told us you was Loyd

Beecham," Cliff said, motioning toward Beecham. "I told him you was Jake Lansford. He laughed and said you like to hide behind names. He said to tell everybody at the ranch they had til sundown tomorrow to leave. He said we had to ride and keep riding. After sundown tomorrow, nobody is leaving unless they are dead. That's just how he said it. He wasn't loud or mean. He said it as calm as a leaf floating in the creek." Cliff paused for a moment and looked hard at Beecham. "He said you ain't leaving at all."

Beecham's face was as white as a fresh snow and his eyes were shifting in every direction. He backed nervously into the shadow of the house.

"Did you see anybody with him?" Garron asked.

"Nope," Ross replied.

"Well, it looks like you'd better get our money ready Beecham. This ain't going to be as hard as we figured. He's come right to us and all we got to do is tree him and kill him," Burl Isom said.

"Let's don't do anything crazy right now," the always careful Wiley Pounds said. "Maybe we ought to send a couple of men back to where the Partains met up with Haddok and see if they can pick up his trail. If he's alone, he's holed up someplace. There ain't no way one man can tie up this whole ranch."

Before anyone could respond to Pounds assessment of the situation, there was a loud crack of a rifle round slamming into the wall of the ranch house, startling and freezing the whole crowd. It was followed a couple of seconds later by the boom of the big rifle. Men dropped in every direction, getting themselves out of any line of sight.

"Where did it come from?" Garron screamed.

At the sound of the blast, Beecham had scurried on his hands and knees through the door. He was flat on the floor inside when he yelled out, "I think it came from the road."

Then a second round hit the house, followed by the sound. Then another. The men were trying to get a fix on the shooter. They saw no smoke or muzzle blast. The sound echoed off the hills and the buttes behind the house. It sounded like it was coming from every direction. They knew it had to be out in front of the house somewhere.

All the rounds hit the house and the last was only about a foot wide of the door. The men hugged the ground for about twenty minutes.

"Sounds like a buffalo rifle, don't it?" Ross Partain asked.

"I think he's gone," Isom said from under the porch.

"I think so too," Garron added. "Horton, why don't you and Walls work your way out to the first high ground and see what you can find out."

They began to venture a move here and there. Benton and Walls stood up to follow Garron's suggestion, but they had just started toward their horses when another slug hit the house followed by the telltale boom. They burrowed back into hiding.

"He ain't gone yet," Walls chuckled. "He's just having some fun with us and there ain't a dang thing we can do about it."

20

Haddok quickly headed to his camp, dropped off the big rifle, and rode out for Fort Defiance. He figured the boys on the ranch would stay holed up for the rest of the day.

He got into town in the middle of the afternoon and headed straight for the sheriff's office.

"Sheriff Bowles, I've started to tighten my grip on the Two Buttes ranch," Haddok said as he walked in.

He told the sheriff about spotting the two hired hands from the ranch while they were in town.

"I waited on them about thirty minutes up the road. When they showed, I got the drop on them and explained how dangerous it was going to be on the ranch. I gave them til dark tomorrow to get out. I told them to tell Beecham and his gunslingers I was coming for them. When I let them two gents go, I hightailed it back to where I could watch the ranch. They showed up with my message and I waited a spell before I started scattering some slugs from an old fifty caliber I got. I put them all into the ranch house. I could tell by my eyeglass them men were in no mood to do any moving around. I figured I had the rest of the day to come back here and fill you in," Haddok said.

"What do you think they'll do?" the sheriff asked.

"I think them that ain't gunslingers will run," Haddok replied. "The rest, they'll stay and I'll have to kill them. Money brought them here and money will keep them here."

"Well, you be careful, boy," the older sheriff said. "I'll help you any way I can, but there ain't a lot I can do unless they break some law around here."

"I know that and I don't expect you to ride this bronc. I would appreciate it if you keep your ear to the ground for me. I'd like to know if any of them gunfighters come to town. It would sure help me if I could get them separated so I could thin them out a mite."

"I'll be glad to do that. You ride careful," the sheriff said.

They shook hands and Reed headed back to his camp. He had a few days provisions packed so he didn't need to stop before leaving town. He thought about his camp as he rode. It would be hard to beat. It was close to the ranch and it was hard to find. He was counting on the gunslingers being more the kind to hang around town rather than the woods. Most of their kind didn't cotton much to roughing it. If he was right, the camp would be safe. If they found it, they would have to make so much racket getting to it there was no way they could slip up on him.

It was getting close to dark when he slipped into camp. He chanced a small fire for some coffee and cured meat. After eating and cleaning up, he set in to thinking. He needed some other way to stir the pot on the ranch. If they were looking over their shoulders all the time, then they couldn't spend a lot of time looking for him. He'd keep his word. He would give them until the end of tomorrow to leave. After that, somebody was going to die. He wanted them gunslingers to know killing wages were always too cheap when you don't live long enough to collect them.

He rolled up in his blanket and slept well, waking every hour or so to check his horses and make sure everything was calm. He stirred the fire up and made some more coffee just a little after first light. Warmed by the coffee, he walked out of camp, leaving his horse this time.

He moved quietly, taking his time, until he got to the vantage point where he had shot at the ranch yesterday. It took about an hour on foot. He stayed well back in the shadows of the trees and glassed the ranch. Smoke was rising from two chimneys and there was movement of men and horses around the ranch yard.

Unknown to Haddok, the Partain brothers and the other men who had been on the ranch when Beecham arrived had ridden out during the night. They had pulled up at the outskirts of Fort Defiance and hailed a man chopping wood outside his house. It was still dark. The man, a fellow named McPeters, watched them when they left and then headed to the house where Sheriff Bowles lived.

He rapped loudly on the door. In a few seconds the door latch was raised and the sheriff stood there, looking half asleep.

"What the devil you want this time of the morning?" the sheriff asked. His agitation was clear.

"Had a passel of riders come by my place just a little while ago. They wanted me to give you a message," McPeters said.

"Well, go ahead. What is it?"

"They first said for me to get word to a man named Haddok that they was riding. The man doing the talking said he would know what it meant. I told them I didn't know nobody named Haddok. It was then they told me to come tell you. They looked a little skeered and didn't want to stay long at my place."

"You did right in coming McPeters. I know Haddok and I'll tell him. You can go on home now," the Sheriff said. He watched the man walk out into the dark. He then grinned a mite and thought, the boy knows how to fiddle up a dance.

21

"Beecham," Garron yelled as he banged on the door. "Come out here. We need to talk to you."

Beecham slowly came out of the ranch house and stood back in the shadow of the porch. The seven gunslingers he had hired to protect him were standing together on the ground just beyond the porch. It didn't go unnoticed to the gunmen that Beecham had the look of a man who hadn't slept much.

"Looks like all your hired help rode out during the night," Garron said. "I put them Partain boys on the gate for the late guard duty. Seems liked they used it as their chance for the whole lot to ride out."

"They wasn't worth nothing anyway," Beecham replied. "They'd just get in your way. Now you won't have to work around them."

"We've been talking, Beecham," Garron continued. "You've had a twenty thousand dollar bounty on Haddok's head for a spell. So far, nobody's collected. We hear that some pretty tough folks have tried. Now, here we are in the same place as them gents. We don't aim to desert you. What we want is your top dollar. This is all about money to us. It's all about Haddok to you. We know we can kill him. We also know some of us might die in the doing. We want to know your top price and we want it to go to whoever's left when we're through."

"We made a deal," Beecham said.

"From what we've heard and the best we can count, there's about twenty-five men you've made deals with and you ain't spent a dime yet. Now, if you don't like it, we'll ride out," Garron said.

Beecham didn't like it. His face got red and he muttered a few cuss words under his breath. He started once to go back in the house and let them leave. His better judgement got a hold of him and he turned back to look at them. "Okay, this is my top price. Fifty thousand to be divided between whoever is left."

"That's good enough," Garron said. "You try to mess us up after he's dead and we'll kill you. You understand?"

"I won't try nothing. I just want him dead and it can't happen soon enough."

Garron turned to the men. "Benton, I want you and Harper to work your way over to the tree line. Check out the high ground over there that would give Haddok a clear shot at the ranch. We all think that's where the shooting has been coming from. Look for any sign. If you find any tracks, trail them. We've got to start putting a little pressure on him."

"That won't be hard," Benton Walls said. "You want us to go ahead and kill him if we find him or do you want to drag this out?" Walls smiled as he asked the question.

"You know what we want to do. The rest of us will work out a way to defend the ranch for now," Garron replied.

Walls and Harper left to saddle their horses. They rode back behind the ranch house and then turned west. They held as low as they could until they got to the tree line. They started south from there, carefully checking the ground for any sign.

Haddok had his glass on them when they left the ranch yard. They dropped from sight a couple of times. They're headed for the trees, he thought. They're starting the day looking for me. Maybe I'll let them find me.

Haddok moved his glass off the two men and went back to study the ranch. There was no other movement. He didn't want to focus on the two men on his left and let the others work their way around to cut him off. Assured no one else had left the ranch, he went back to observing the two riders. They were in and out of the trees, moving slowly toward his position.

Garron couldn't have picked two men with less experience at reading sign. Walls and Harper were both stand up gun fighters. They were good at it. They had spent little time trailing anything. They were working slow, doing the best they could. You could tell they were a little nervous because they stopped often to look all around them. They really didn't have much of an idea what they were looking for. Outside a clear hoofprint or shell casing, it was unlikely they would find anything.

"I ain't seen a thing. Have you?" Walls asked.

"Nope. I say we just keep moving. Maybe something will show up," Harper answered.

They continued to work their way south, getting serious a couple hundred paces from Haddok's position. They dismounted and walked slowly, leading their horses. Haddok lowered himself down in some brush about twenty paces inside the tree line. He remained very still and watched them as they worked their way past. Their heads were turned away from him. He raised up and took about five quiet long strides and stopped directly behind them. The sound of the hammer clicking back on his pistol jolted both men. They whirled to look down the barrel of a pistol being held by a man who appeared to be so calm he could be eating chicken at a church social.

"Now ya'll be real careful," Haddok said. "Somebody's going to die here if you don't"

"You got the drop on us mister," Harper said. "No need to start shooting. We ain't crazy."

"I understand you've been hired to kill me," Haddok said. "I might as well know who you are."

"I'm Wade Harper. This here is Benton Walls," Harper said as he cut his eyes toward Walls. Walls was coiled on the edge, ready to draw at the slightest opportunity. It just so happened Haddok's pistol was pointed at him, not Harper. "We're from Kansas."

"I sure hate you men tied in with Beecham. He uses people like they were something you buy off the shelf in a store," Haddok said casually.

"We got no need to do any shooting," Walls said as he spoke for the first time. If it started, he knew he was good as dead from what he had heard about Haddok and the fact the man's pistol was already in his hand and pointed right at him. "You let us ride and we'll head for Kansas."

"I don't reckon so," Haddok said. "You hired out your gun and if you've survived this long in the Kansas wars, I figure you to be pretty good. If I let you ride, you'd show back up. The money would keep you here. The man who hired you would shoot you in the back if he had the chance. I ain't that kind of man. I'm going to holster my pistol and you can start up whenever you feel like it."

Both men dropped the reins of their horses and held their hands in clear view, waist high. They didn't know what the other was thinking, but both thought this feller must be pretty sure of himself to do a fool thing like he just said.

"That sounds fair enough," Harper said. "Under different circumstances it might have been good to ride with you."

Haddok smiled as if he had no care in the world. "There ain't no condition I know of that would put us riding together."

Haddok had been busy reading the two men. Walls was faster but Harper would be the hardest to kill. He didn't know how he arrived at that decision. He just did. Walls would get the first bullet and Harper the next two. He also knew they would be looking for an edge. It suddenly dawned on him their edge would be when he put his pistol in it's holster and raised his hand back up. They would drop theirs as his hand came up.

It was deathly quiet as the men stood facing each other. Then a gentle breeze, just for a moment. Haddok thought, Death's old fiddler is warming up the strings. In one swift move, Haddok lowered his pistol into the holster and drew it right back out. He fired three quick shots as the gunmen went for their pistols. The first shot hit Walls in the chest and threw him backwards. The next two caught Harper in the chest. He managed to get one round off, but it went harmlessly into the air. Harper was dead. Walls was dying. Haddok walked over to look into the face of the young gunman.

"You're good," Walls coughed as he was dying. "Didn't know you was that fast. Should have known."

Haddok quickly rounded up their horses, slung their bodies across their saddles, tied their hands and legs beneath the horses, and then he did something he hadn't done in a spell. He pulled his knife and sliced off the right index fingers of both men. He threw the fingers into the brush, wiped the blood from his knife blade, and sent the horses running back in the direction they came from. He then left out of there at a fast pace, careful to leave no sign.

22

The men back at the ranch had heard the shots. The sound brought the five remaining gunmen and Beecham out into the yard. They shielded their eyes and tried to see anything moving.

"Go get the money ready Beecham," Isom said. "Benton Walls and Wade Harper are two of the fastest men with the draw I've ever seen. I'd bet my horse they found Haddok and laid him out. I never figured making the money would be this easy."

"I've never seen Harper in action, but I've been with Walls in three shootouts. I'd lay my cards on him any day," Wiley Pounds added.

They were now in a festive mood, jawing with one another and eyeing the southwest tree line. Beecham never said a word, staying inside the shadow of the house.

"Look yonder," Melton shouted. "They're coming."

They could make out two horses, but it didn't look right. It got quiet as they dispersed from their tight knot and settled into the cover of the buildings and a nearby wagon. Beecham stepped quickly back inside the house.

After what seemed like an eternity, the horses walked slowly into the ranch yard and stopped, heads hanging. Isom eased out to get the rains and walked between them as he headed for the barn. The rest of the men, including Beecham, met him there. They lowered the bodies of the dead men to the ground and rolled them over on their backs.

"One shot in Walls heart and two in Harper"s chest you could cover with a dollar," Isom said.

"I knew both these men," Garron said. "They were good and wouldn't neither one give up in a fight. They were both shot in the front. I think we just learned why the price is so high on Haddok's head."

"If he's too good for you, then I guess it's best we find out now," Beecham said.

"Didn't nobody say anything about him being too good," Garron replied. "The deals still on and we'll collect. We'll just have to be careful how we corner him so the edge will be ours."

"Look at their hands," Isom said.

Melton chuckled. "I'd heard he did that to some of your gunfighters out at Prescott. Didn't much believe it. Why would a man cut a dead man's finger off?"

"I don't think it's funny Melton. I tell you one thing right now. When we corner him and the shootings over, the last one of you standing better keep him from cutting my finger off. I plan on meeting my maker with all of them," Garron said.

They took the bodies and buried them behind the ranch house. They were quiet as they worked. To a man they understood why Benton Walls had one slug in him and Wade Harper two. Harper would still be shooting with only one in him. It told them Haddok was more than fast or good. He was a gunfighter. That title only belonged to fast good men who were smart. All five felt a little uneasy. None would have admitted their feelings.

23

Haddok made it back to his camp a little before dark. It took longer afoot. He had been careful not to leave any sign. He waited until way after dark to risk a small fire back under the overhang. The coffee was good. He didn't cook anything. He was afraid the smell might give him away. He chewed on some jerked beef and savored the hot coffee. His horses had fared well during the day while he was away. He fed them some grain and moved them around a little before dark. His plan was to be up early and back on the high ground overlooking the ranch by first light.

He made it to his place overlooking the ranch and was down low in his position glassing the ranch when the sun came up. He felt like the deaths of the two men would make them be a little more careful. He kept a close vigil on the ranch and saw no one leave or enter. He had noticed movement around the ranch and it was obvious they were not staying out in the open for long periods of time. He spotted one guard position on the high ground behind the ranch house and there was one man off to the side of the main ranch house. One man had entered the ranch house right after daylight and another left. He figured they were keeping at least one man inside at all times. The other two stayed out of sight except when they changed places with the two outside guards. Haddok saw Beecham for one brief moment when he walked out on the porch, but he quickly went back inside.

Haddok's mind was running full out, thinking of ways to play with their minds. He wanted to get them so worked up they would jump at the chance to confront him. He had a plan. The thing he wanted to do right now was push them and push them hard. He knew the kind of men they were and he knew they were not accustomed to hiding and taking water from any man.

While he waited and watched, he thought of something that might twist the rope a little. He took Partlow's rifle and sighted in the door to the main ranch house. He had to add some elevation because of the distance. He had figured out just how much from his previous shots at the ranch.

Comfortable with his sight pattern, he put the rifle down and went back into the trees and found a bush with some straight limbs. He cut four, trimmed them, and sharpened one end of each. With the prongs lowered on the front of the rifle barrel and the stock solid against his shoulder, he sighted in the door of the ranch house again. When satisfied, he took one of the small limbs and stuck the sharp end well into the ground right up against the barrel. He pushed it into the earth deep enough for it to be stationary. He then pushed another into the ground back against the action of the rifle, just in front of the trigger guard. He sighted it carefully and holding it in place, he marked the height of the rifle on the limb with his knife. Lowering the rifle, he carefully cut the limb at the marked height. He placed the rifle back into the sighted position and saw that when the rifle barrel was against the front limb and the stock was against the back limb at the exact height of the limb, the door of the ranch house was the precise target. He moved the rifle away and returned it several times and checked the sight pattern. Perfect.

Next he sighted in the bunkhouse where the gunmen were sleeping and repeated the procedure. When he had the limbs in place, he removed the rifle and returned it several times to make certain he had a good sight pattern on the bunkhouse. When he was satisfied, he went back to glassing the ranch. He would save the surprise of the day until after dark.

When nightfall finally came, Haddok put his eyeglass up. The last movement he had seen was the guard coming down from the high ground behind the ranch. They were keeping a tight circle of defense.

Haddok gave them enough time to get settled in before he placed the big rifle up against his aiming stakes. He snuggled in behind it. He was going for the ranch house door first. He laughed to himself, knowing the rounds from the rifle would go through the walls of the ranch house and bunk house. He envisioned bullets bouncing around inside and men diving for cover.

Comfortable everything was lined up, he gripped the cocked rifle strongly and squeezed off the first shot. Even in his strong grip, the big rifle bucked against his shoulder. He checked to see if his sticks were still in place. They were fine. He switched positions to the bunk house sight pattern. As soon as he was lined up, he squeezed off another round. The sound echoed off the high ground around him. He repositioned the rifle for a second shot at the bunk house. As soon as he was ready, he let the big rifle bark again. He moved back to the ranch house position and fired one last shot. He then quickly gathered his sticks and rifle, heading back to camp. He thought, I'd like to be down there and see how those boys like being holed up with lead bouncing around.

Beecham, Isom, and Melton were in the ranch house when the door shattered. Split seconds later they heard the boom of the rifle. They doused lanterns and crawled around on the floor, putting anything they could find between them and the front wall.

The second shot seemed to have missed. Then they heard yelling from the bunk house. They then knew it had been the target of the second shot.

The first bullet into the bunk house had grazed Garron's leg. The men in the main ranch house could hear him cussing. Then it got quiet. Beecham and Isom were discussing whether or not somebody ought to go check on them when the second round hit the house. The bullet hit the fireplace and ricocheted across the room.

"Anybody hurt?" Melton asked.

"I'm okay," Beecham answered.

"Me too," Isom said. "But I didn't ride this far to crawl around on the floor in the dark. Come daylight, I'm gonna find that man and kill him."

At that moment there was a rustle outside and Garron announced they were coming in. The three from the bunk house slipped in quickly and crawled toward the other men's voices.

"Are ya'll all right?" Garron asked.

"We're fine," Isom answered. "How bout ya'll?"

"That first shot grazed my leg. It came clean through the wall with no trouble. Wonder what he's shootin?" Garron said.

"I'm wondering more about how he's shooting. It's black dark out there and he's parting our hair," Isom said.

"You know, I'm sure proud ain't nobody here to see this," Melton said. "I ain't sure I ever seen you boys crawlin afore. Could be this Haddok don't respect us like he oughta."

Isom laughed at the thought. "Unless you can see in the dark, you ain't seen me crawling, so don't go off and tell it that you did."

"This ain't funny," Garron replied. "If you think it is, then your leg feels a lot better than mine."

24

Haddok had a plan to get the gunslingers off the ranch so he could deal with them. He returned to his camp, saddled his horse, and headed out for Fort Defiance. It was getting on toward midnight when he walked up on the porch of the sheriff's house.

Haddok rapped on the door several times and waited. The sheriff soon answered, pistol in one hand and lantern in the other.

"Come in boy," the sheriff said. "You're traveling mighty late."

"I'm sorry to get you out of the bed," Haddok said. "I've been stirring the pot a little at the Two Butte ranch and I think they are about ready to come looking for me. I had me a run-in with two of Beecham's gun hands yesterday. They were a might slow and I killed both of them. "

"You have been busy. I had a bunch of men who came through here a few nights ago saying they were leaving the ranch. They wanted me to get word to you."

"I knew they were gone. It plays into my plans. I need a favor. I'd like to ask you to ride out to the ranch and set the bait for me."

"What you got in mind?"

"I want you to tell them about the men who came through town the other night wanting to get word to me they were leaving. Then say that was the first you had heard about me being anywhere around. Make it sound like you don't want my kind around your town and you were afraid I was causing trouble out at their ranch."

"What else?"

"Play it up like you would be willing to help them if they need you. Be sure to ask them if I have broken the law in any way on the Two Butte."

"Is that all you want me to say?"

"Nope. I want you to drop the news that I've sent word to you setting up a meeting with you at ten o'clock in your office day after tomorrow."

"So, you are wanting them to come to town," the sheriff said.

"Yep. I might as well get this over with. They're hanging so tight around Beecham what I'm doing now could go on forever."

"Son, you're talking about going up against five men. Are you crazy?"

"May be. I figure I'm good for three of them if I get a little lucky. I hope they'll leave at least two to look after Beecham," Haddok replied.

"What if they all come and Beecham comes with them. That would be six."

"I don't believe Beecham will come and I don't believe he'll let them leave him alone. We'll just have to wait and see. It all depends on them taking the bait and coming to town. The one thing you could do for me here in town would be to get some help and keep an eye out on how many do come in. I need to know that. I don't want somebody laying up to backshoot me."

"I can do that and I'll be proud to help you," the sheriff said.

"You will also need to alert the people in town to clear off the streets and get out of the way on that morning. Whatever will happen will happen out there on the street. I hate to bring this kind of trouble to your town. Just remember, if I don't deal with Beecham and his men, then you will have to sooner or later."

"I ain't got no problem with you taking them on here in town. I just wished I could put together some people to help you. To be honest, these people ain't cut that way and I'm getting so old I ain't much use in a gun fight. But I can cover your back and I'll be proud to do it."

"I appreciate it Sheriff. If you could ride out that way early tomorrow and break the news to them, we'll just wait and see what happens," Haddok said.

"I'll do it," he said. "Will you come back into town tomorrow?"

"I probably will tomorrow night. I'll be laid up watching the ranch when you ride up. Be careful. I'd make sure I had my badge in plain sight and I would ride out in the open so they don't think you are nosing around. It's possible they could start shooting before they know who you are. I think I've got them pretty skittish."

They shook hands and Haddok left to head back to camp. He'd have just about enough time to get there, eat a mite, and walk to the high ground overlooking the Two Butte.

25

"Somebody is comin down the road," Zeke Melton called over his shoulder as he shielded his eyes and tried to make out the rider. He was yelling to Isom and Garron who were positioned close to the ranch house. Melton was on guard duty at the gate.

"Keep him covered and we'll walk on down there. Don't take no chances. Haddok might just do what we wouldn't expect him to do," Isom said.

Isom and Garron moved on down to the gate, doing as much as possible to keep from being out in the open for long. They got there a little before the rider reached the gate. As he rode up close, Melton had his rifle casually in the direction of the man.

"Howdy," the rider said. "I'm Eli Bowles, sheriff of Fort Defiance."

"Howdy Sheriff. My name is Isom and these two fellers are Garron and Melton," Isom said as he motioned toward the others. "What brings you this far out of town?"

"I'm just doing a little checking and trying to figure out what's going on. I had a bunch of riders come through town during the night a couple of days ago. They left a message for me. They said they had been working here on the Two Butte and they wanted me to get word to a man named Haddok that they was leaving and wouldn't be back. From what they said, seems like they had run up on Haddok somewhere out here and he had spooked them. I reckon the whole country has heard about Haddok and to be perfectly honest, I don't want his type hanging around my town."

"We had some men to leave all right, but we didn't know why," Garron answered.

"What I'm trying to find out is whether or not Haddok has been causing ya'll any trouble. If he has, then I'll have a reason to put him on the road or behind bars," the sheriff continued.

Isom and Garron looked at each other with puzzled expressions and Isom answered. "No, he hasn't caused us no trouble. Matter of fact, ain't none of us ever seen Haddok."

"Well, I wanted to find out before tomorrow. He sent a feller to my office yesterday and set up a meeting with me tomorrow morning. I wanted to find out all the facts before I met with him. If he's causing trouble around here, he's about to find out this place won't stand for it."

"I wonder what the meeting is all about," Garron said, trying to get the sheriff to talk. It's kind of strange him wanting to meet with you, all the trouble he's been in. That is if all the talk is true about him."

"I don't know. The feller just said Haddok would be in my office around ten tomorrow. Kind of riled me a little, like I'm supposed to hop when he says hop. I was hoping you folks could give me a good reason to run him out of the country," the sheriff said, acting his part perfectly.

"We're sorry we can't help you Sheriff," Isom said. "Won't you come on up to the house and set a spell?"

"Thanks, but I'd better ride on back. If I can ever be of any help to you folks out here, give me a shout," the sheriff said as he turned and rode off.

The three men watched until the sheriff was out of sight. Then they had them a back slapping good time as they hustled back up to the ranch house to tell Beecham and the rest the good news.

26

Meanwhile, changes were in the wind back at the ranch on the Brazos.

Jake Haddok had sold out and he and his daughter Tess were now on their way to the Rocking H. They had been on the road for over four weeks. They were traveling with four packhorses and three Mexican men Jake had hired.

He sold to Raul Sanchez, a Mexican friend who had been only one of three people who knew the real identity of the infamous Doc. He was a trusted friend and that fact alone overcame the only problem he had leaving. His wife Sarah was buried on the place and Jake knew Raul would look after her grave. He sold the place lock, stock, and barrel. The only things they kept were on the four packhorses.

Jake knew the day was coming when his gunfighting days would be over. He also knew there was no way for Tess to ever meet enough men to find a husband the way things were. He also had a desire to be close to his son. He had left out of there with enough money in hand to buy him a place in Arizona and settle down to serious ranching.

Tess was excited about the change in her life. She had a special relationship with her brother and had missed him terribly. They had grown close after their mother's death and did most of the ranch work together while their father was away. It had been like another death when Bud rode off. She couldn't wait to see him and to meet his woman. She knew Samantha had to be quite a lady to capture Bud.

The travel west had been uneventful. They rode from first light until a little before dark each day. They encountered few travelers and no Indians along the way. Jake had traveled the route a number of times and knew how to ease through the danger points.

It was mid-morning on their thirty sixth day on the trail when they rode into Prescott. They spent the night there after paying the Mexican men and sending them on their way home. The next morning they headed north toward the Rocking H ranch.

A ranch hand had spotted them and announced that company was coming. Josh, Raven, and Samantha rode out to meet them, accompanied by three other riders.

"It's them alright," Josh said as he recognized the visitors.

"Howdy folks," Doc said as he dismounted. "I'm Reed's father and this is his sister Tess."

"I've told them we've been friends for a long time," Josh said as he swung down to shake Doc's hand and slap him on the back. He hugged Tess and introduced himself.

"I'm Raven, Josh's wife," the beautiful counterpart to Josh's life said as she walked over.

"And I'm Samantha, your new kin folk. I tried to get Reed to wait until you got here to get married, but he wanted to go ahead. He's been gone about three weeks. He headed to Fort Defiance to try and track down Loyd Beecham."

"Did he go alone?" Doc asked.

"Yep," Josh replied. "He wouldn't hear of letting me go with him. We've been keeping wraps on the ranch. I kinda think it's a waste of time though. We ain't had anybody show up for a spell trying to get Reed. You know how he is. He always gives me that talk about being better off alone. Says he don't have to worry about nobody else when he's alone. Makes me think of somebody else I know."

"I know who you are shooting at now Josh. I guess he does

come by that honest." Doc said. "You better help us get Tess settled in somewhere. As soon as we do, I'm heading for Fort Defiance. I may need to help my boy."

27

Doc traveled all day and into the night, only stopping when he was too tired to go on. He knew the route and was comfortable moving after dark. The thought of his son facing a bunch of hired killers caused him to care less who saw him along the trail. He pitied the man who tried to stop him.

He made good time and rode into Fort Defiance about mid-morning on his seventh day out. He headed for the livery where he put his horses up and shucked the duster he always wore on the trail.

"Give them a good bait of grain and rub them down for me," Doc said to the hostler. "They've earned it."

"Sure thing mister," he replied. "If you'd let me give you some advice, I'd suggest you just stay in here with me for a spell."

"Why?" Doc asked.

"We're fixin to have us a shootout I think. The sheriff told us to clear the street about ten o'clock and it's about that time."

"Who's doing the shooting?" Doc asked.

"A man named Haddok is meeting with the sheriff right now. There's supposed to be some gunmen from out at the Two Buttes ranch show up after Haddok."

"You don't say," Doc said. "Maybe I'll just take your advice and stay in here to watch it with you."

"Suits me. I just didn't want you to walk into anything and get shot," the hostler added.

"That's mighty neighborly of you. Could you point out the sheriff's office for me?"

The hostler led him to the wide double doors and pointed across the street. It's the building on the corner. Right over there. It's the one with the wagon out in front."

"I see it. You say this man named Haddok is in there with the sheriff right now?"

"Yes sir. Saw him meet the sheriff out on the walk and go inside. At least I figure it's who it was. I've never met Haddok."

Doc thought about the situation. He knew his son. Reed wouldn't be treed in no building if he didn't want to be. His son was doing the treeing. The wagon brought a smile to his face when he saw it. It was there on purpose. He could tell by the way it was pointed and with the tail gate out. Reed probably had him some back up weapons in the wagon. He wished he knew how many Reed would be facing. It didn't matter though. They'd just have to sort out whatever shows up.

"Which way you figure they will be coming from?" Doc asked.

"The Two Butte is north. They will more than likely be coming from that direction," the hostler said as he thumbed the direction up the street.

Doc thought, they'll have to come by me. I believe I'll just sit tight and see what my boy is up to. He stood back in the shadows of the livery and looked north. His senses picked up to a trot. He saw five riders slowly coming into town. They stopped about five buildings to his right and hitched their horses. Then they moved out into the street and carefully headed toward the sheriff's office. They were checking the windows, doors, rooftops, and any other place where somebody could be laid up for them. Without thinking, Doc reached down and flipped the loop off the hammer of his six shooter. He picked it up in the holster about an inch and let it ease back down. He was ready.

28

Reed Haddok seldom went within himself to consider his own feelings. He was a man who lived his life and all it's uncertainties with a set mind of doing whatever he had to whenever he had to do it. He was raised that way and it was normal for him to live his life that way. He didn't get to choose what tomorrow would bring. He did get to choose how he would deal with it. If it was raining, he lived with the rain. If a cow was calving and the calf was breeched, he rolled up his sleeves and pulled the calf. If one man or a bunch of men got in his way of doing what was right, he moved them. It was a simple way of living.

But here he was, on the night before his planned showdown with Beecham, and all of a sudden his life didn't seem that simple. He admitted to himself that he didn't want to die. He had looked death square in the eye on numerous occasions. It had never bothered him before. Why now? Her name was Samantha.

The short time he was with her after the wedding had been wonderful. He relived it over and over again. For the first time in his life he had a real reason to live. Oh, he had friends and family. They meant the world to him. But Sam. She was the person who had thrown and hog-tied him. It was so different now. He wanted to live.

As certain as he knew that, he also knew it was entirely possible he wouldn't be alive by tomorrow night. Five good gunfighters were a little too much for one man to handle. He had a rare thought. Nobody would ever know of it, because he would never tell. He thought seriously about saddling up and riding out of Fort Defiance. The thought did not prevail. He quickly replaced it with the full knowledge he had to deal with Loyd Beecham now. He could not afford to let him get close to Sam.

In the brief time he remained within himself, he simply resolved to be faster, tougher, and more determined to win than the men he would be facing. He knew he would get shot. He would just have to keep shooting until they were dead and then hang on for help. Seemed like he had spent way too much time hanging on here lately.

In a flash he stepped outside his mind and started doing what must be done. Three pistols and two rifles were thoroughly cleaned and their actions checked. They were loaded and set aside. He then stretched out to sleep. His mind was set. He knew what he had to do. He slept well.

29

The street was deserted except for a few stragglers scurrying into doorways. There was the smell of dust in the air. The day was clear and the wind still. A dog barked somewhere and a door slammed. The gunslingers heading toward the sheriff's office were cocky. To a man they knew they were good. This would be short work. They were determined to rid themselves of Haddok and collect their money.

Burl Isom was in the middle. He was flanked by Garron and Wiley Pounds. Toby Horton was on the left flank and Zeke Melton on the right. They walked by the livery door. Doc peered out of the shadows and saw the faces of the men. He knew two of them. He smiled when he saw Melton. The cold feeling of indifference spread through Doc's body as he looked at the back side of five men intent on killing his son. He again checked the loop on his pistol and lifted it a little to let it lightly settle back down. He was about ready to walk out and join the party.

The hostler had been watching the gunmen, but suddenly became aware of the stranger's actions. He has all the looks of becoming a player in the shootout, he thought.

Reed and Sheriff Bowles knew when the gunslingers arrived. A rider had come with the news that five men were coming in from the north.

"Well, I got lucky," Reed said. "I won't have to worry about any more of them after this morning."

"You are plumb crazy, boy," Bowles said. "You ain't got a chance against five gunslingers."

"Oh, I don't know," Reed replied. "If it was just me, I'd figure you was right. All my life I've found myself in situations where the odds were against me and there's this man who rises up inside of me and takes over. When it's all over and the dust settles I usually can't remember a thing except being alive to walk away."

"Oh, son. You are as crazy as a betsy bug. When does this man usually show up?"

"He's been here for about an hour now," Reed said, smiling. "Thanks for arranging for the wagon. The pistols and rifles in the back of it will help. And I may need to dive in behind it." He slapped the sheriff on the shoulder and walked out the door.

Haddok's abrupt appearance on the boardwalk stopped the gunslingers dead in their tracks about twenty-five paces from the sheriff's office. Haddok walked down onto the street and behind the wagon to stand in front of the five men.

"You gents here to kill me?" Haddok asked.

"That's what we're being paid to do," Isom said.

"Well, what are you waiting for. I wouldn't want the word to get out that I drew first and had an unfair advantage on you boys." Haddok grinned and it completely disarmed them. Men in his circumstance don't grin. They sweat and are nervous. This man was not sweating. He was as cool as ice on the creek. "Whenever you get ready to die, start shooting."

"Just a minute," Isom said. He didn't know why he said it. For some reason he wasn't ready. "How did you kill Harper and Walls? Was it a fair draw?"

"If you mean did I give them a chance to draw, the answer is I gave them the same chance I'm giving you. They were just a mite slow." Haddok was busy trying to decide who to shoot first. He settled on the young one on his left and the tall lanky one on the right. The others would just have to come as things worked out.

Isom was about to respond to Haddok when a deep, calm voice spoke from behind them.

"Zeke, you a long way from home ain't you?" Doc asked. He was settled behind the gunmen, about twenty paces off.

Melton turned his head and shock registered on his face. "Doc, what are you doing here?"

"I heard a bunch of gunmen were after my boy so I rode up to see if I could help," Doc said.

Reed recognized the voice and let his eyes pop up for a split second to see his paw standing in the street with a tied down six gun hanging on his side that looked almighty comfortable there. The gunslinger called him Doc, Reed thought. Oh my.

At that moment, Melton lifted his hands slowly until they were chest high. "Boys, I'm out of this. Doc let me walk one time in Missouri. I was just a kid. I saw him take four men I thought was good. Only reason I'm alive today is he let me walk. Doc, if you'll let me, I want out."

"Ain't my call , Zeke. You better talk to the man standing in front of you. I hear he's a mite faster than his paw."

Things were not working out for the gunslingers. They were edged in between two fast guns and one of their own was trying to quit.

"If you stand real still, I won't shoot you," Reed said to Melton. "Now for the rest of you, let's get this thing over with."

"What if I decided I want out?" Wiley Pounds asked quickly. He was the only one of the five who always checked the odds and his were way down on being alive when the shooting stopped.

"Nope," Reed shot back. "Paw, which one do you want?"

"I thought I just might take whoever has his back to me," Doc chuckled.

In an instant Isom and Garron turned to face Doc.

"I've always wondered what would happen if you ever showed up in a town where I was," Isom said.

"Why, I must have misunderstood what happened in Kansas a while back, Burl. The word I got was you left out the same day I arrived in Burnout. You should have hung around to find out," Doc said with a go to hell carelessness.

"That's a lie," Isom said.

"We ain't here to talk," Reed said. "Ain't none of you leaving alive. If you don't want to start the dance, we will. Believe me, your chances are better if you do."

Doc faced Isom and Garron and Reed stood in front of Horton and Pounds. It was getting hot. There was no breeze. Death was dancing all over the place. It was the young Toby Horton who went for his gun first.

The fusillade of shots that filled the air were so rapid you couldn't count them. When Horton went for his gun, Reed instinctively drew and fired a shot into his chest. He remembered hearing a shot a split second before his. He thought, Paw ain't slower than me. After he fired into Horton, he shifted his position one step to the left, firing as he moved. His second and third shots hit Wiley Pounds. He stepped sideways and fired a fourth shot into Horton. All four of the gunslingers were down. They cleared leather, but none of them got a shot off at the father and son. Reed and his paw had each fired four times and the four dead men had two chest wounds each.

Through it all, Zeke Melton stood motionless. Reed walked over to him.

"How much was Beecham paying for my hide?" Reed asked.

"Fifty thousand," Melton answered.

"Where's Beecham?"

"At the ranch."

"I tell you what I'm going to do," Reed said. "I'm going to give you a chance like my Paw. You can ride and I'll make it my personal goal in life to kill you if I ever see you again. Or you can ride to the ranch, collect your money, and bring me Beecham's dead body by sun-up tomorrow."

"Fair enough," Melton said. Turning to Doc, he said, "Honest Doc, I didn't have no idea he was your kid. I wouldn't have been here. I've always owed you and I ain't forgot it."

"He didn't know he was my kid either," Doc said with a grin. "Oh, he knew I was his paw, he just didn't know what I've been doing for a living all his life."

"I sure didn't and we've got a world of catching up to do," Reed said. "Zeke, that's your name?"

"Yep."

"Be careful. Beecham is pure mean. He carries a gun tucked in his belt and he has a hide out derringer," Reed said.

"Thanks, I'll bring him and then I'm gone to Kansas."

Melton walked to his horse on weak legs, swung into the saddle, and headed north for the ranch. He felt lucky.

30

Reed and Doc got some men to drag the bodies away and they paid for the burial. Sheriff Bowles told them he had never witnessed anything like their gunfight in all his days. He asked the men to eat lunch with him and they spent an hour or so in the café. As soon as they could get away, they went and rented a room with two beds. They had a lot to talk about.

"Paw, I can't believe you handled being a gunfighter so me and Tess never knew it," Reed said.

"It wasn't always easy. I never intended for it to become my way of life," Doc said. He took the time to explain about his first killing and then how protecting Reed's grandfather caused him to kill again. "After that, I had a name with a gun in Missouri and the word spread. I never used the gun except for the right cause. The money was good and people kept on asking me to help them deal with lawless people in their towns. When we moved to Texas, I thought I could get away from it, but it followed me. Times were rough on the ranch and I was barely scratching out a living for ya'll. I never wanted to go off and leave you, especially after your mother died."

"Did Maw know?"

"Yes. She was one of the reasons I never talked about it with you. She didn't want you to know."

"Did you come to Prescott?"

"Yes. But when I got there you had already cleaned it up."

Reed was full of questions and it was almost like a kid putting a puzzle together. "Did you kill Will Malone?"

"Yes I did. Would have killed Beecham too but he had already flown the coop."

"You mean you've been out there all this time covering my back and I didn't even know it?"

"No I haven't son. You've been on your own. I'm mighty proud of you. I never wanted you to live my kind of life. I can see now you couldn't help it any more than I could. It is my fault though. I raised you to be like you are. You found yourself with a job to do and you did it. Now you'll have to live with the reputation you earned."

"One more thing. Tell me about Josh. He's talked a lot about being a friend of yours. I'm beginning to think you had something to do with him showing up when I headed off the Brazos."

"You got me figured right boy. When you left home, I got in touch with Josh and asked him to find you and make sure you stayed alive til you learned the ropes. Me and Josh go way back. He's stood with me in some tough scrapes and is the closest friend I have."

"You mean he's been my nursemaid," Reed said with a laugh. "You wait til I see him."

"Don't be rough on him son. He was doing your paw a big favor."

"Oh, I won't. He's my best friend too. It all makes sense now. Josh is the reason I'm alive today. He taught me how to handle a pistol and the fast draw."

They talked on until time for some supper. After eating, they went back to their room and turned in. Both men were exhausted. They went to sleep with the joy of knowing there was plenty of time to get caught up on their talking.

They were awakened the next morning with a knock at the door and the sound of a ruckus down on the street. Sheriff Bowles yelled through the door.

"Ya'll better come on down and meet Loyd Beecham."

They buckled on their pistols and followed the sheriff down

the stairs. When they walked outside they were confronted by a crowd of town folk. Zeke Melton was setting his horse in the middle of them. Melton held the reins of another horse. The body of Loyd Beecham was draped across the saddle.

"Here's your man," Zeke said.

Reed walked out to him and lifted Beecham's head and looked into his dead eyes. "You've done your job and you saved me from having to do it," Reed said.

"When I rode up at the ranch, he was waiting on the porch," Melton said. "I lied a little because it ain't in me to just ride up and shoot a man. I told him the others were dead and we had killed you. When I told him I wanted my money, I figured him to be the kind of man who would kill me to keep from paying. He led me inside and brought out this sack. I ain't ever seen so much money. I guess he figured seeing the money would take my mind off everything else. I acted like it had and he went for that little old pistol he carried in his vest pocket. He gave me a good reason to kill him."

Zeke looked over at Doc. "I hope there ain't no hard feelings Doc." He then tossed a large canvas bag to the ground. "There's the money. I just got what I had coming. He owed me two hundred dollars. I've done a lot of bad things in my life, but stealing ain't one of them." Zeke scratched his chin and continued, "Well, I did steal a apple pie off a winder sill in a little ole town in Kansas one time. I was hungry and had some people on my trail. Went back by there a while later and paid the woman. She didn't want the money. Said she would have give me the pie if I had asked her. I made her take the money. Felt better."

Doc grinned. "You just got to find another way to make a living," Doc said. "Sooner or later I'm gonna have to kill you if you keep this up. Tell you what. I'm going back to Prescott and start ranching. Why don't you ride down that way later and look me up. I'd rather kill you with hard work than shoot you." Doc was smiling at the rough gunfighter.

"Now that's a thought, Doc. While I was riding out to the

ranch to get Beecham, I spent some time thinking about that very thing. I mean getting away from hiring out my gun. I said, Zeke, old boy, you are just a few minutes past missing a good chance to take that ole long dirt nap. Doc, them fellers you and your boy killed were good. People in most parts of the country who knew them was afeared of em. I told myself, Zeke, you been riding with some tough men, but they're dead now. To be honest Doc, I think your boy could have took us all. When you showed up, well, he was twice as good. I said to myself, Zeke, you better find you somethin else to do."

"My offer stands Zeke. If you decide to take it, ride careful when you get to Prescott. Tell anybody you talk to that I sent for you. They don't take kindly to anybody trying to kill my boy around there."

"You got yourself a hand," Zeke said. "I'll be seeing you." He dropped the reins of Beecham's horse and rode out.

"Sheriff, see that he's buried," Reed said as he handed him some money. "I'm taking this money with me." He picked up the canvas bag. "It ain't for me. He beat a lot of people out of their money around Prescott and I aim to see they get repaid."

They shook hands and the two men went to gather their gear and head for the Rocking H ranch.

31

The trip back to the Rocking H was a nine day pilgrimage of new discoveries and old memories for Reed. The shock of learning his paw was the infamous Doc, gunslinger and tamer of lawless towns, gradually wore off and his desire to learn all he could about the side of his paw he did not know kicked in.

They rode long days at a easy pace and camped early enough to insure their safety and seclusion. They stopped before nightfall, had an early fire to cook supper, let it die down to coals by dark, and sat around enjoying the coffee and talking. They were skilled at hiding their camps and protecting themselves.

The first night around the dying fire was typical of every night along the way. The day had been spent with alert and careful riding. There was no talking. Not so around the fire.

"What did you think of Samantha?" Reed asked.

"She's a beautiful girl and I could tell right off she's got some backbone in her. I'm proud for you Bud," Doc replied.

"She's an amazing person Paw. She can ride and handle a horse as well as any man I've seen. She's tough and I'm not sure I'd want to get in a shooting match with her."

"I didn't meet her father. What kind of man is he?"

"He's a great man. He's strong and has built one of the finest ranches around. The Diamond covers a lot of territory. It's well run and he's got the respect of every man who works for him. You will enjoy meeting him. Ya'll are a lot alike."

"When I rode to Prescott a while back I rode out to the Diamond to talk with Josh. It's a fine spread."

"I still can't believe you were here and you didn't talk to me."

"I did see you. I had to before I left. I rode over to the Rocking H after you ran Beecham off and saw you and Samantha from a distance. You were perched on a piece of high ground overlooking your ranch. Looked a whole lot to me like you were courting." Doc laughed across the coals.

"You are about to make me mad Paw," Reed said with a chuckle.

"It was hard on me not to talk to you. I just didn't want you to know your old man was a gunfighter. I always wanted a different life for you."

"I'm proud of you Paw. I understand now more than ever before how a man can get started in that kind of life. You were just doing what had to be done and you happened to be good at it."

"You got to believe me when I say I didn't plan a life of a hired gunman."

"I believe you. I also believe all your work has been for a right cause. I can understand you better because I never planned on killing a man with a gun. But then I had never met a man who needed killing. I've tried not to kill unless I was left no choice. The men I've killed have earned it. Still, I don't like it. It's amazing how you can get kinda pushed into it. I'd just as soon never have to face another man in a gunfight. Maybe Beecham's death will put a end to this crazy mess."

"I hope so Son, but don't count on it. You've got a name now and killing seems to follow the name. It did for me."

"I hope I can handle it as good as you have if it does. Tell me about Tess. Was it hard for her to leave the Brazos?"

"It was hard for both of us. We spent most of the day before we left by your mother's grave. We felt like we was leaving a part of us there. I didn't tell her, but it was really hard for me. I kind of had the feeling I would never be back."

"You really loved Mama didn't you?"

"More than I could ever tell you. I hope you and Samantha always have what we had. She was a special and tough woman. She made me the man I am."

"Did Tess make the trip okay?"

"Oh sure. She's better than any man around. One of the reasons I wanted to come this way was a hope she might find a decent man to spend her life with. Wasn't much to pick from on the Brazos. I didn't tell her that. Course I ain't seen a man yet she couldn't whip in a stand up fight. Most menfolk shy away if they ever see her riled."

Reed laughed. "I know what you mean. I'd sure hate to have to fight her."

"She's grown into a beautiful woman Bud."

"Sam will be good for her. Maybe she can help us smooth her out some."

"Maybe so."

"You got it in mind to find a ranch to buy?" Reed asked."

"Yep. If I can. I got some money saved up and I got a pretty good price for the ranch when I left. Have you found anything I might be interested in?"

"You probably won't have no trouble finding one. I would rather you take your time and make sure before you buy. Me and Josh own the Rocking H together. Sam's father has been trying to get me and Sam to move in at the Diamond and take over. He got roughed up by Beecham and it took a lot out of him. I ain't talked serious with him about it. I'd want to know he's ready to slow down. I don't want to be the reason he hangs it up. If we move in over there, or stay at the Rocking H, there will be a place for you and Tess until you get settled in.

"Boy, I ain't ready to move in permanent with you yet," Doc

said with a smile. "I got a lot of horse left under me and I aim to settle down and do some serious ranching. It'll just be good to be close by."

"Somehow I didn't figure you was ready for me to be your boss," Reed said, laughing.

32

It was getting late on a Sunday when Reed and Doc rode up to the Rocking H. A crowd spilled out of the bunkhouses and main house to meet them.

Reed swung down and handed the reins and lead rope to one of his ranch hands. Sam threw her arms around him.

"Is it over?" she asked.

"Beecham's dead and the job is finished," Reed replied.

"Did you kill him?" Sam asked. All ears were tuned to their conversation.

"Nope. Didn't have to."

"What do you think about this mean old Sis of mine?" Reed asked Sam as Tess threw her arms around him.

"I think she's great. She's already told me how to handle you," Sam said, laughing.

Josh and Raven pushed their way through the crowd. The two men looked each other in the eye. "Is he dead?" Josh asked.

"Yep." Reed replied. "He had seven gunslingers close around him. I got two of them early. I baited the five he had left to come into town and catch me in a meeting with the sheriff. They took the bait and I was just about to get chewed up when this old Texan named Doc showed up. Paw knew one of the gunfighters from way back. He begged out when he saw Paw. We took the other four in a gunfight. I offered the one who begged off a deal. He could ride, but he had to bring us Beecham. He brought him the next morning, stone cold dead."

"I'm proud it's over Bud," Josh said. "Maybe now you can settle down."

"I hope so. Ya'll got anything to eat? Me and Paw are starved."

"Come on into the house," Sam said.

Reed and Doc stood off to the side with Josh while the women got some food on the table.

"Josh, you've got some explaining to do," Reed said. 'Paw tells me he sent you to look after me and by the looks of the mess I've been in since I left home, you ain't done much of a job." Reed was enjoying this.

"Boy, there ain't enough men in Texas to keep you out of a mess," Josh said, slapping him on the shoulder.

"I really do owe you for being there for me Josh. I wouldn't have made it without you."

"I owe you too," Doc said. "I was telling Bud you were my closest friend. I'll always be grateful."

"Ya'll are making me feel bad. Hush this mushy stuff. If I hadn't come out here, I wouldn't have a ranch or a wife. Tagging along with you has been a right profitable thing for me."

"All the same, it's good to have you as a friend and we both owe you," Doc said. .

"I appreciate the thanks, but I've got something on my mind that's mighty worrisome," Josh said.

Reed and Doc frowned.

"This house is gettin mighty full and I don't know where we'll all sleep," Josh said, laughing.

"I been thinking on that myself," Reed said. "I figured me and Sam would head for the Diamond tomorrow. We'll take Paw and Tess with us. You can handle things here til we get Paw settled in somewhere."

At that moment, Sam called them to the table. When they

finished, they moved to the porch where they talked through the sunset. During a lull in the conversation, Sam took Reed's hand and led him off to the corral fence where they held each other for a long time.

Then Sam looked up into the shadowed eyes of her husband. "Reed, we need to build that house we've been talking about."

"I know. Maybe I can spend some time on it now."

"I don't want to rush you. I just want to have a place of our own before our child get's here," she said.

"What did you just say?"

"I want a house of our own," she said, giggling.

"I don't mean that. What did you say about a kid?"

"We're going to have a baby."

"Boy or girl?"

Sam laughed. "I can't tell you that. We'll have to wait and see."

"It'll be a boy I know," Reed said as he squeezed her tight. "I'll be dog. I'm gonna be a Paw."

33

Eleven months later Reed Haddok was sitting by the fireplace on a cold February night. Sam sat across from him with Joshua Tree Haddok at her breast. The fresh cured wood burned hot, popping and sending sparks up into the chimney. The flickering of the flames caused flashes of light in the dark room.

His thoughts went to his mother. He then thought of what life would hold for his son. He looked at the glow in Sam's eyes as she gazed down at the baby held close. This was why he crawled out of bed with Sam for the nightly feeding. He usually threw a couple of logs on the fire and sat quietly, watching the two miracles of his life.

On this night, he thought of his future. He was forever changed by the series of events over the past three years. No matter what happened from here on, he knew he would have to live the rest of his life on the edge. It was the price he would pay for doing what's right. He knew, without hesitation, he would do it again, given the same circumstances.

Then he thought of his son. It was a great responsibility to have a son. The very thought was heavier than any weight he had ever carried. What will I do, he thought? A smile, unnoticed by Sam, broke across his face. He had heard it so many times he didn't miss a word. He whispered the words, "Boy, I better not ever hear of you causing trouble for no man, woman, or child. If I do, I'll tan your hide. But if trouble ever comes your way, you don't cut it no slack. If you have to fight, always remember that it's them that keep gettin back up that win. You just keep gettin back up til you see quit in his eyes."

Reed knew he was a man today because his Paw raised him to be one. He made up his mind right then that there would be another man to wear the name Haddok. Joshua Tree Haddok. He liked the name. He already knew the man who wore it, even though he looked a whole lot like a baby at the moment.